Stef had fierce dominant tendencies, and she loved nothing more than to order a submissive around, with the spankings and cruelty that resulted when orders were not followed exactly. She had had her own submissives in the past, but once she started working at Rough Trade, she decided that it wasn't worth the trouble. Rather than commit herself to one or two submissives, and the time and effort required to keep them in line all the time, she simply got her fill from the clientele at the bar. Sometimes submissives would come in on their own, and Stef would pounce on them. But she preferred situations like this, where a Mistress was more than happy to share. This one seemed as if she wanted to, and Stef had jumped at the chance.

Also by LINDSAY WELSH:

nasty persuasions

LINDSAY WELSH

ROSEBUD

First Rosebud Edition 1996

First Printing September 1996

ISBN 1-56333-436-4

Manufactured in the United States of America
Published by Masquerade Books, Inc.
801 Second Avenue
New York, N.Y. 10017

Chapter One

The late-afternoon sun streamed through the large curtainless window, moving slowly across the floor and along the bed as the antique schoolhouse clock on the wall ticked away the minutes.

The clock chimed four times as the sunbeam reached the cheek of the woman sleeping in the huge bed. As it did, Slash woke up.

She opened her eyes immediately and then stretched luxuriously, pushing aside the snowy white sheets. She had no need of an alarm; her internal clock was as uncannily accurate as a Rolex. She was in complete and utter control of her body, just as she was in absolute control of everything else.

Stretching again, lithe and feline, she got out of bed. She slept naked; her body was flawless, and she paused for a moment to look at herself in the mirrored wall that faced the bed. Her stunning appearance made passersby stop and admire her on the street; when she moved through Rough Trade, women threw themselves at her feet.

She was slightly over six feet tall, thin and deliciously sinewy, each muscle clearly defined through years of aggressive workouts. Her skin was the color of finest bittersweet chocolate. Her tits were hard, upright globes, the nipples huge even at rest; her stomach was firm and flat; her mound was covered with curly black hair, the treasure under it moist and ruby-red. Her close-cropped hair accentuated the razor-sharp features of her face and her impossibly high cheekbones. To call her beautiful was not enough. Slash was simply and utterly magnificent.

Preprogrammed, the coffeemaker had turned itself on earlier. Walking naked into the kitchen, Slash poured herself a cup of the bitter black liquid and looked out the window. The New York street below her second-floor window was busy as always, and the relentless sound of the city came faintly through the thick glass. No one looked up at her, no one saw her standing there completely nude with her coffee in her hand, but if they had, Slash would not have cared.

She lived alone in this huge loft, on the top floor of the two-story warehouse occupied below her by Rough Trade. It mirrored her diverse and mystifying personality, with its bare, rough, sandblasted brick walls and its mirror-finished smooth wood floors, with its heavy wooden antique furniture and ultramodern appliances. A claw-footed copper bathtub shared space with a six-person whirlpool. A professional kitchen that would have been the envy of a hotel chef was lit by converted gas lamps, but all of it was superfluous because Slash never cooked at all. She had wanted it, and so she had it.

Whether or not she used it was completely beside the point.

All of it was possible only because of Rough Trade. Slash had worked long and hard at it, weathering lean years and investing wisely in good ones. Now she owned every inch of the huge nightclub laid out below her.

It was definitely the best-known club in all of New York, arguably the most famous in the country. Possibly every dyke in America had heard its name.

If Slash had been a multimillionaire, she couldn't have bought the advertising that Rough Trade received by word of mouth. Women talked about it, magazines mentioned it constantly. Lesbians conversing with each other on the Internet raved about it even if they had never been inside its doors.

For New York women, it was a regular spot. Midwestern lesbians took part-time jobs to save up enough for a trip to the Big Apple and a chance to visit it. West Coast women wrote long pleading letters to Slash, begging her to open one in San Francisco or Seattle, sending tempting photographs of themselves as bait.

It was hyped and all but enshrined, and it might have collapsed under its own weight but for one thing. Women who heard the stories about what went on behind that heavy steel door, stories so fabulous and fantastic that they could only be fiction, visited and came back with the astonishing news: it was all true.

It was due to Slash's three rules regarding the bar. Anything was acceptable, entertainment had to be rough and outrageous, and it had to turn her on personally. Since Slash's sexual cravings were almost insatiable and open to just about everything, any night at Rough Trade was guaranteed to be unforgettable.

Her coffee finished, her dark body still unclothed, Slash walked through the loft to her training room. Here were the devices she used to keep herself in such shape, and with the late afternoon sun behind her and the radio blaring, she spent half an hour exercising, until her skin shone, burnished with sweat. She enjoyed a quick shower and then opened the door to her huge walk-in closet, with its relatively small collection of street clothes, and its three racks of tightly packed costumes that she wore both while working in Rough Trade and during the rare occasions when fortunate women were invited back to join her in her loft and her bed. Everything imaginable from satin suits to leather and chains hung neatly, waiting to enhance her perfect lines.

This early in the day—for excitement at Rough Trade generally started at nine, and finished long after the first rays of dawn—she put on an oversized T-shirt and nothing more. It only helped to emphasize the length of her legs and the darkness of her skin.

She poured another cup of coffee, opened the door to her private staircase, and slowly descended into the silence of the huge, darkened rooms of Rough Trade.

No matter how many times she walked downstairs before opening, it always seemed strange and almost eerie for the bar to be so quiet. In the evenings, the nightclub was a riot of activity, packed with women no matter what night of the week it was. The babble of voices would be almost overpowered by music, the darkness stabbed by colored lights. Women would be embracing, grinding against each other. There would be sexual activity in the high-backed booths, in the corners, sometimes right in the middle of the nightclub floor between patrons so carried away in the moment that it didn't matter that a roomful of women were watching—

or sometimes, it was everything that all eyes were on them. There was always a live sex show put on by Slash on the enormous hardwood dance floor. The whole room would smell of sex and desire.

Sipping her coffee, looking around at the club, the huge room lit only by the sunlight that got around the mass of neon signs in the small windows, Slash could hardly wait for nightfall and the sexual tension, raw hunger, and satisfied cravings that would begin when the first leather-clad patron walked through the door and end only in the early morning, when Slash would call closing and lock everything up behind the last of the revelers.

There was a metallic click; the huge steel door opened slightly and then closed. Slash, who very seldom smiled, grinned and said, "Morning, Ramone."

Ramone called out a greeting in return and walked into the silent bar, her footsteps echoing through the cavernous room. As she did every afternoon, she stopped, took a sip from the cardboard cup of coffee she carried, and looked around at the club with a satisfied look on her face.

Like Slash, she was gorgeous. Slim, well-built, her long black hair falling straight to the middle of her back, her face bore the unmistakable almond eyes of her Japanese ancestry. Her skintight jeans and short-cut T-shirt showed off a body as finely tuned as Slash's, the skin creamy and taut across her belly, her tits smaller than her tall companion's but just as firm and uplifted. Unhampered by a bra, her nipples stuck out as hard pips through the thin fabric of her shirt. Like Slash, she was the envy of every woman who walked through the door, and she never lacked for women who would beg to please her.

She was the only woman other than Slash who had ever held a key to the big front door. As Slash's oldest friend, she held the position of assistant manager in the bar, the only one Slash trusted enough to leave in charge on the very rare days she allowed herself time away.

She was also one of the very few who really knew Slash, who knew the woman behind the icy exterior. She was one of the few who regularly used the private stairway up to Slash's loft. She was also the only woman whom Slash had ever given herself over to totally, in screaming orgasms that left both of them weak and sweaty, in nights of mutual pleasure that lasted long after everyone else had gone home.

She stopped to adjust a chair, to straighten an ashtray on a table. Slash was calm and businesslike, Ramone polite and efficient; it was a game they often played together in these quiet moments before opening time.

"Did that keg of beer that I ordered come in?" Slash asked, busy looking over a pile of receipts.

"It came yesterday," Ramone said as she put her coffee down on the bar, "but I haven't hooked it up yet." She appeared to be checking the huge display of liquor bottles behind the bar, but really was watching Slash out of the corner of her eye. She could see Slash's already-huge nipples all but pop out of her T-shirt and her mouth watered at the thought of Slash's ruby cunt, all hot and eager for her. Even without thinking, she let her hands drop. Her fingers unbuckled the heavy belt that surrounded her waist.

The jangle of the large chrome buckle was all that Slash was waiting for. In a moment, she was on top of her, and their mouths met in a frenzy of hunger.

The taller black woman bent down to the Japanese woman. Their arms moved around each other, hands sweeping over skin in long caresses. A slinky movement from Slash's fingers sent Ramone's shorts to the floor around her ankles, exposing her pussy. Ramone's hand moved under the hem of Slash's shirt, and she moaned loudly through the kiss as she grabbed Slash's bare asscheeks. They were rockhard, smooth as glass. Slash spread her legs apart and Ramone's fingers slid into the crack in between.

Now Slash was groaning, too, as Ramone found the hot, slippery cunt that was waiting for gratification. It was so juicy that Ramone knew that in a minute, the hot, thick liquid would be running down the inside of those exquisite thighs, and she puddled her hand between Slash's cuntlips to flick a knuckle over the firm nub of Slash's clit.

Slash was so horny that the very air around her seemed to heat up. Her tongue was deep in Ramone's mouth and her hands were under her lover's shirt, her fingers massaging the incredibly hard nipples. Both of them were panting, their bellies on fire, their cunts throbbing hard between their legs. "Do me!" Slash whispered.

Ramone needed no further encouragement. In a moment, she was on her knees on the floor, and Slash had pulled her shirt over her head and thrown it away. She stood with her legs far apart, a drop of her sweet cuntjuice threatening to fall from a tightly curled black hair.

Ramone was right there. She used the very tip of her tongue to rescue the drop of precious fluid, and she savored its sweetness.

But Slash was in no mood for gentle love; her cunt was too needy for that. She wanted hard sex; she wanted to come. She bent her knees and pushed her pussy into

Ramone's face and, at the same time, she reached down and pulled Ramone's chin up to her, grinding Ramone's lips into her cunt.

Ramone responded immediately. She wanted Slash's cunt as much as the tall black woman wanted to be eaten. Her tongue pushed aside the fleshy lips to get at the wet delicacy under them. Slash's cunt was as firm as her body was, the folds of skin ripe and sex-swollen. Ramone loved to burrow with her tongue to Slash's clitoris, to run her tongue over it and push it from side to side and play with it.

She did it now hard—and fast. Her tongue flashed over the clit as she sucked the juice from Slash's cunt. She thought her mouth would overflow with it, there was so much, and it was hot and sweet as it ran down her cheeks. One hand was at Slash's hole, probing with a finger. When Slash moaned, Ramone put in a second one, then a third. She fucked Slash's hole hard and fast with her hand, her knuckles disappearing into the velvety depths, the juice running down her arm, as she ate Slash's pussy with an intensity that was shocking.

"Fuck my cunt!" Slash groaned. Her hips were bucking back and forth on Ramone's lips; she couldn't hold still. Ramone shoved into the velvet tunnel and pulled back out. Her fingers were sopping with juice and slid back inside effortlessly. She sucked Slash's clit hard, then licked again. Her tongue was flashing over Slash's pussy.

"Fuck me! Fuck me harder, honey!" Slash's mouth was open, and she was panting. The whole club seemed to be filled with the rich perfume of her pussy. Ramone was pushing up from the floor, trying to get in as deep as she could. Her whole face was buried in Slash's cunt, her hand deep in Slash's hole.

The tremors began deep in the tall black woman's

pussy, radiating out into her belly and finally through her entire body. She groaned and then began to cry out in short bursts as she came. Ramone rode her out to the end, her hand covered in pussyjuice to the wrist, her face soaked with fluid.

Slash was not in the mood to bask in the afterglow. In one swift movement that amazed Ramone, she spun around and picked up her lover under the arms and lifted her up until she was sitting on the bar. She was tall enough that she was at Ramone's height, and her mouth was on her lover's in a flash.

Ramone returned her kiss as hungrily, their tongues pressing against each other. The bar reverberated with the husky sound of their moans. Slash's hands were busy. One was on Ramone's tit, kneading and squeezing the huge, hard nipple. The other was between Ramone's legs. Ramone spread her knees wide and Slash was into her pussy seemingly up to her wrist.

Ramone wanted it as hot and hard as Slash had. Her bare ass squirmed on the polished bar as she ground her cunt against Slash's hand. Her own hand was on her other tit, and she was squeezing the nipples hard. The pain crossed back and forth over the threshold of pleasure, and when she knew what was happening, Slash pinched hard as well. She was fucking Ramone with her hand, with her tongue, with her fingers. She wanted to get right inside Ramone, and Ramone wanted her there.

There was a wine bottle on the bar, still corked, and Slash took her hand away from Ramone's pussy long enough to grab it. Her nectar-soaked hands left wet streaks on the glass bottle. Her tongue still in Ramone's mouth, her fingers still on Ramone's tit, she used her free hand to press the cork-tipped bottle end against the fleshy, soaked lips of Ramone's cunt.

As fluidly as a finger, the bottle sank into Ramone's hole.

Ramone gasped and kissed even harder as the glass bottle penetrated her. The wine sloshed in the bottle as Slash fucked her with it, rhythmically, gently. It was not enough. Ramone grabbed the bottle, too, and pushed it deep into her cunt, the neck disappearing, groaning at the delicious fullness inside of her.

Together they fucked her with the bottle. Then Slash let go of Ramone's nipple and found the clit that was so swollen with want it seemed it would explode. She rubbed it, pushing it against the bottle as it went in and out. It was too much for Ramone, who began to tremble and then screamed out her pleasure.

When they removed the bottle, they held it between them, and both of them licked the hot, sweet pussyjuice from the glass. Then Slash pulled out the cork and took a long swig of the sweet wine, passing it to Ramone, who did the same. After being passed back and forth twice, the bottle was empty, and Slash plopped it down on the bar with a satisfying bang.

Their urgent needs met, they returned to their business, rearranging their clothes and going back to what they were doing. Ramone hooked up the beer keg, while Slash checked the supplies of clean glasses and towels.

"What's on for tonight?" Ramone asked, as she straightened up from under the bar and wiped her hands clean.

"I have those two coming in who do the routine with the dildo," Slash said.

She said it so matter-of-factly that Ramone had to laugh. It was always this way. When the bar was quiet, when they were alone and Rough Trade was just a business spot opening for the night, to Slash the acts were just entertainment that she had booked for the evening, with no more regard than if they were simply musicians or comedians. But Ramone knew that once everything got under way, when the bar was filled with dykes in leather and Mistresses with submissives at their feet, with gorgeous women wearing nothing more than straps and chains and couples eating each other out in the back booths and the rooms kept open for them, she knew that Slash would be anything but matter-of-fact. She knew all too well that once those two women were on center stage, one wearing a rubber cock slung low on her hips, the other spread on a chair begging to be fucked wide open with it, the tall black bartender would be eyeing up the crowd, looking for some young thing to order to the floor, to service that delicious ruby pussy and then be tossed back into the crowd.

Slash knew it, too. When she caught Ramone's eye, she smiled herself.

"You busy?" she asked as she threw the clean towel down onto a chair.

"Not at all," Ramone replied, and the two of them walked arm in arm to the private staircase at the back of the room. Rough Trade didn't open for several more hours. There would be plenty of time to get everything else done.

Chapter Two

"A Scotch and two beers," Cherry said, and she put her tray down on the bar and looked around the crowded room while she waited for Slash to fill the order.

Cherry was Rough Trade's headwaitress—Slash and Ramone worked the bar expertly while Cherry waited tables and supervised the other servers. She stood on one leg, bending the other to work out a stubborn cramp.

It was hard work; there were no slow nights at Rough Trade. It was, however, the single disadvantage of the job.

She couldn't begin to list the benefits. That night, when she had come to work an hour before opening, she had been greeted with kisses and a grope from both Slash and Ramone, as she had every time she came in for work. It was not unusual for two of them, or even all three, to end up in a booth, in one of the rooms in back, or upstairs in Slash's loft either before or after the evening—or sometimes during the long nights when one or the other could slip away from the bar for a few minutes of sweaty, fevered sex.

As Cherry looked around, she couldn't help noticing some appreciative glances come her way from women either sitting at the bar or standing nearby. It was very easy to understand. She was fairly tall, very well built, and her shorts showed off perfect legs while her shirt stretched nicely over firm breasts. Her hair was dyed bright red, smooth and silky, cut on a sharp angle with her jaw. Unlike many of Rough Trade's patrons, who had the pale complexions of night people, Cherry was tanned and robust. It only added to her appeal.

Cherry was not her real name; no one knew her real one. It didn't matter. Most of the regulars figured she came by it because of the shocking color of her hair. Slash and Ramone knew that it was from her love of deflowering virgins. No one had ever come close to breaking as many cherries as this insatiable woman had.

Now, as Slash put the three glasses on the tray, Cherry reached over and let her hand stray to Slash's arm. They touched for a brief moment, and Slash gave her a rare smile. Cherry knew her almost as well as Ramone did, and Slash's pussy grew warm at the thought of her redheaded barmaid. "Later," she promised, and Cherry smiled back in return. Her cunt was just as hot.

Cherry turned and walked through the noisy, crowded bar. There were women everywhere. Cherry couldn't help staring at one woman who was wearing nothing but a pair of leather panties and thigh-high black leather boots. Her nipples were huge, and when she saw Cherry looking, the blonde squeezed them and then pushed them out invitingly. Her tits were big, and she bent down and licked one of her own nipples with the tip of her tongue, then looked up at Cherry and offered them again.

Cherry, her cunt already hot, was suddenly aware of the throbbing between her legs. She nodded and then turned to the three women who had ordered the drinks. She set them down almost absently and then turned. The huge nipples were still being held out like candies. "Cover for me, Stef," Cherry called out to another waitress nearby. She then turned and indicated with a nod that the leather-clad beauty should follow her. From her vantage point behind the bar, Slash looked on approvingly. She wouldn't have turned down those tits, either, and she was almost sorry she hadn't noticed them first.

The blonde followed Cherry through the crowded bar. Several women turned to stare at her, and one reached out a hand to brush the hard, uncovered nipples as they passed.

The blonde spun around so quickly that the other woman didn't even see her move—until her wrist was caught in one strong fist and pulled back behind her head. Their eyes met, the blonde's cold orbs staring down the startled look of the transgressor. They stood like this for several seconds. Then, without a word, the blonde tossed the wrist away, violently, and continued walking behind Cherry. The other woman watched for a moment, then, shamed, melted back into the crowd.

Cherry walked to the end of the bar, into a dark corner behind the row of pay phones. One was in use; the woman, who wore skintight jeans and an open denim jacket with nothing under it, never even glanced at the two as they stepped into the shadows. Cherry dropped her tray on the ground and turned to face the half-naked blonde.

The blonde again offered up her tits in both hands.

Cherry bent down and took one of those perfect nipples in her teeth. She could feel the blonde shiver just a bit as she did, and the tiniest sigh escaped her lips, but no words were spoken.

As she sucked and licked the nipples, Cherry reached down and unbuttoned her own shirt. Her unfettered tits fell out, the nipples just as big and hard as the blonde's. Her mouth filled with tit, Cherry sighed herself as she felt the blonde's red-lacquered fingernails brush the very tip of her left breast. The chill went right through her body. Then the blonde kneaded it between her fingertips and cupped the breast with her hand. Cherry's body heated up, and she could feel her pussy juicing up with want.

She was waiting, every muscle in her body quivering, for the other hand to move down. When it did, Cherry could feel the nub in her mouth grow even harder. The probing fingers found the small gold ring that went through her right nipple, and when she stood up, the blonde traced the designs of the dragon tattoo that made its way from the tit right up to the shoulder.

Cherry was proud of her ring, excited by the blonde woman's reaction, but she had an even better surprise in store. She stood up straight and unzipped the shorts, pushing them low on her hips so that her bush was exposed. Then she took the blonde's hand and led her to the searing heat between her legs.

She felt the fingertips playing with the hair and tracing designs on the skin. Cherry's hand was on the impossibly huge nipples in front of her, the other slipping just inside the waistband of the leather panties. She thrust her hips forward, impatient for the blonde to find the surprise.

When she did, the other woman sighed happily in

Cherry's ear. Gold rings, adorned with tiny pearls, went through holes pierced in her pussylips. There were two, one on each side, sunk deep into the meat of Cherry's cunt. The blonde touched them both together; Cherry could smell the delicious perfume of cuntjuice and leather as the blonde's own cunt responded. The blonde now thrust her own hips forward, and Cherry took up the invitation. Her hand moved within the musky confines of the black leather panties. The cunt she found was shaved clean, slippery with thick, rich juice. Cherry's fingers slid across the smooth skin as if they were greased and came to rest against the hard lump that grew in size against Cherry's hand.

They were locked tightly together. Their breasts were jammed against each other, their fingers were deep in each other's cunts, but their faces were over each other's shoulders. They did not look at each other; they did not kiss. At that moment, the steam rising from her cunt, her fingers sopping with the blonde's juice, Cherry could not even remember what the woman looked like. All that mattered were the fingers playing with the rings in her cunt, the hand that was brushing on her clit, and the other hand that was between them, squeezing her nipples alternately.

The blonde woman came first, panting hard, groaning. It set Cherry off, and she sighed long and hard as the waves of pleasure passed through her body. They clung to each other tightly, shivering, their fingers moving hard to squeeze the very last of the orgasms from each other. Then it was finished, and they stepped back, trying to catch their breath.

Neither of them spoke a word. Cherry zipped her shorts and buttoned her shirt. The blonde adjusted the black leather panties; her nipples were a bright rosy color, and her breasts rose and fell magnificently with her heavy breathing. Cherry turned around to pick up her discarded drink tray. When she stood back up, the blonde was gone.

The woman dressed in denim was still talking on the phone; she glanced up as Cherry walked by, but that was all. She had had the redheaded waitress herself, under similar circumstances, several weeks before. But if Cherry recognized her, she did not show it; and the denim-clad woman merely looked, and then returned to her conversation.

"Thanks, Stef," Cherry called to the backup waitress, who smiled and nodded. Covering for Cherry meant running her legs off, but Stef didn't mind at all. She was just as likely to request the favor herself, if a particularly promising woman smiled her way and looked ready to be taken back behind the pay phones or into the rooms at the back.

The rooms were four small cubicles, originally designed for storage, that were behind doors near the washrooms at the back of the bar. Slash had emptied them and two of them were fitted with small cots, just large enough for two women to lie down—perhaps with one or two women on top of them. Two larger rooms were outfitted in a much more sinister fashion. They had heavy tables in them, tables perfect for throwing a submissive woman over and clamping her firmly to the legs. There were also rings set into the walls, at various heights. Many a terrified submissive had spent a long night shackled to those rings, either crouching on the floor, standing as comfortably as they would allow, or hanging from the rings that were placed just below the ceiling, too high for any chained submissive to stand.

Even now, Stef was sizing up the women she was

serving. There was one single woman, sitting alone at a small table, who was leaving huge tips with every glass of beer that she ordered. There was another, standing against the wall, whose shirt was opened just enough for Stef to see a leather bra under it. But the ones who intrigued her the most were a couple sharing a table. By the taller one's cold smile and the smaller one's bowed head, it was obvious that this was a Mistress taking her submissive out for the evening. Stef was very open that night to the thought of standing beside another woman and putting a slave through her paces.

For now, though, all of these would have to wait. Two of the waitresses were setting up that night's floor show.

One nodded to the disc jockey, a rail-thin woman known as Kiki, with several rings through her nose and ears and one gold ball pierced through her tongue, who stood in her booth by the door. At the signal, she waited until the song was finished and then turned down the system. Reluctantly, the women on the dance floor walked off of the polished hardwood. The music would return, loud and pounding, once the entertainment started up.

The two waitresses brought over a long, padded piano bench and set it in the middle of the huge empty floor. It was a very sturdy one, with thick legs and rounded feet. It would have to be; it was going to take a lot during this session.

The room was almost silent with anticipation. Then Kiki started up the music that indicated the floor show was about to begin. The regulars, who knew it so well, cheered.

The music was fierce and pounding, and Kiki turned it up gradually. From deep inside the crowd, a woman walked forward, toward the dance floor.

She was wearing a magnificent silk kimono, and her

blonde hair flowed down the back of it. It was a show, and she was making the most of it. She danced around the outer perimeter of the dance floor, where women were huddled shoulder to shoulder. She stopped to take a long kiss from one, and with another, whose shirt was open, she felt the naked breasts that were offered to her. One woman tried to open the kimono, but the blonde stepped back. It was going to be offered to everyone at once.

She made another round of the floor, until her lips were wet with deep kisses. Then she went to the center and stood on the bench. All eyes were on her as she dropped the kimono.

She was exceptional. Her tits were huge, her mound blonde and fuzzy. She was stocky and well built and she had creamy thighs that every woman there longed to have wrapped around her neck. She lifted up her tits and held them out in offering, then put her hand between her legs. When she held it up her fingers were glistening, and she licked her own cuntjuice slowly from them.

Behind the bar, Ramone looked up at Slash, who was watching her intently. "Nice one," she murmured appreciatively.

"You've seen nothing so far," Slash said. "Wait until they get going." Her own hand was between her legs, and Ramone could see that she was rubbing her pussy slowly. Ramone smiled, wondering who would be ordered to the floor to pleasure that steamy cunt tonight.

The blonde woman lay down on the bench, on her back. Her breasts pointed up and she spread her legs invitingly. It was obvious that several of the women in the crowd wanted nothing more than to rush over and kneel down, to take in the treat so offered, but they held back. Slash's entertainment was always worth waiting for.

As the music grew louder, a second woman walked through the crowd. She was also wearing a robe, this one of bright blue satin. Her hair was short and dark and she was thin, although the robe stuck out invitingly over her chest. Like the blonde woman, she made the rounds of the dance floor, kissing women who were waiting open-mouthed for her, but she did not permit any of them to reach for her.

She walked to the middle of the floor where the blonde was waiting for her, spread on the bench. Moving with the relentless rhythm of the music, watched by hundreds of lust-filled eyes, she reached down to pinch the nipples that were waiting for her. Caught up between pleasure and pain, the blonde woman writhed on the stool and moaned, openmouthed. Slash caught her breath at the sight, and Ramone sighed and reached for her own sopping pussy.

The brunette's fingers went down the pale skin of the blonde's belly, to that white-hot place between her thighs. Her hand stayed there for a long time as she felt up the clit. Then she turned to her audience and waited until the music reached a climax, and she dropped the robe.

The audience cheered in a single scream. The brunette was naked but for a black leather harness that was strapped low on her hips. From her mound thrust a huge, shiny pink cock.

Once again she circled the dance floor, this time holding out the cock as a gift. She stabbed at them with her hips, used it like a machine gun on them. Several women touched it, wrapped their hands around its massive thickness.

Now the brunette spotted a Mistress in the crowd. She held the end of a dog chain; the other end was snapped to the collar around the neck of the naked woman kneeling at her feet. The brunette asked the question with her eyes, and the Mistress smiled coldly and nodded assent.

To the crowd's roaring approval, the brunette stopped in front of the submissive and held the cock out. The submissive, her eyes wide with fear, looked up at her owner questioningly. The answer was given with a rough tug of the chain. With tears in her eyes, the submissive endured the cheers and jeers of the crowd as she took the huge dildo into her mouth and fellated it.

The brunette fucked her mouth with it, choked her with it. Tears now running down her cheeks, the young slave sucked the cock as her Mistress looked on and smiled. The lordly woman's pride was evident as she caught several admiring glances from other dominatrixes in the crowd. It was difficult enough to train a submissive in privacy, but here she had proven that she could command a woman to obey her in the middle of the most crowded dyke bar in all of America.

The brunette stayed there a few minutes longer, until every woman craning her neck over the crowd had a chance to see the submissive sucking on a cock so huge that it distended her mouth. Then she pulled away and moved back to the bench where the blonde, her pussy glistening in the lights, watched and waited.

It was this pussy that the brunette moved toward. The bench was at the height of her hips and so smoothly that it seemed buttered, the enormous cock sank deep into the depths of the juicy blonde cunt.

The crowd of women roared again, some lifting their drinks, others turning to their partners for kisses, or for hands slipped into jeans or between leather straps.

The blonde gasped as the whole length of the huge

cock slid into her. The brunette was teasing right now, getting into it. She lifted the blonde's leg over her shoulder, slipped a hand under her ass to raise her hips, and slowly, lusciously, pulled the cock out and then pushed it back in.

It seemed as if everyone in the room held her breath as she did. Their eyes never left the scene. The whole room was hot and sweaty and smelled of steamy cunts and sex. They loved the way the leather straps rode low on those spiky hips, the way one strap went between her legs and hugged her cunt hard to hold the cock in place. They loved the way her tits swayed with each slow movement, and they wanted to see them bounce when she finally started to fuck that blonde good.

She didn't disappoint them. Writhing on the bench, holding her tits and kneading the nipples, the blonde begged to be fucked. The brunette, still holding one perfect leg over her shoulder, banged her hips hard until they were a blur. She stopped and pushed and pulled the cock slowly, while the crowd oohed, and then fucked again as hard and fast as she could.

Standing at the edge of the dance floor, Cherry was transfixed. She loved the sight of a woman being fucked by another woman, especially the way this lanky brunette was expertly wielding that prick. She was masterful. The orgasm she'd had with the anonymous woman in the corner had only made her eager for more. She simply couldn't ignore the hot spasms in her cunt.

Suddenly she stripped off her shorts and shirt. Slash and Ramone, standing behind the bar, had wondered how long it was going to take. Having Cherry become part of the evening's entertainment was a regular event. The women near her who watched her strip eyed the dragon tattoo and the ring in her nipple with eager anticipation, and when they noticed the rings in her cuntlips, they could have cried for want of her.

She walked over to the bench and, without a word, straddled the blonde's face. Groaning loudly with appreciation, the young woman did not hesitate to first suck the twin rings into her mouth and then push her tongue deep into Cherry's cunt.

The brunette smiled at this turn of events, but she didn't miss a beat, ramming the cock home into that velvety, sopping tunnel. Cherry's pussy was worked over expertly. She leaned forward. The brunette met her mouth. Their tongues were instantly in each other's throats. Locked together, they enjoyed the blonde below them. Cherry's hands were on the blonde's large, creamy tits, massaging the nipples. As the crowd cheered, she shivered with delight. The blonde had found her huge, rockhard clit and was lapping at it. Cherry's hips were moving as fast as the brunette's were. She ground her cunt into the blonde's mouth even as her companion fucked her pussy raw.

Finally, it was too much even for Slash. The tall black woman was wearing only a short skirt, and she lifted it up to reveal her mound, glistening with liquid. When she did, she noticed the look of anticipation on a customer standing near her.

Slash had never seen this woman before. She was a small dark woman wearing a low-cut T-shirt and tight jeans. That didn't stop Slash from pointing to the floor at her feet and ordering, "Suck me!"

The woman was on the floor in a flash. Slash reveled in the hot chills that went through her entire body from her clit. The woman was good; her tongue found the most sensitive places right away, and stayed there. Slash never gave her another glance. Her eyes were on the dance floor, on the blonde stretched out on the piano bench, and on the two women, their mouths locked together, one grinding on her face, the other fucking her with an obscenely huge cock.

Slash knew when Cherry came; she knew the flush that started on Cherry's tits, that covered her chest and went right to her throat as she began to moan. The blonde woman never stopped, and Cherry kept bucking her hips, riding it out. Then, completely satisfied, she kissed the brunette again and left.

Slash grinned. How she loved Cherry's style! It was so like her own; when she came herself a few moments later, she simply stepped away from the woman on the floor.

The woman was puzzled, even shocked, as Slash pulled down her skirt and went back to the bar. "But—" the woman began.

"Go away," Slash replied.

After a long moment, the woman crept away. Slash felt no remorse. For one thing, she was there to take, not to give. For another, she knew that within minutes, the woman would be bragging to her friends that she had been granted the high honor of licking Slash's clit. Any disappointment she felt now would soon be washed away in the glory of what she had done.

Ramone, she noticed, had done exactly the same thing, and now a thin black woman was making her way back into the crowd, licking her lips to get every last taste of the Japanese woman's delicious pussy.

They looked out at the floor. The brunette had finished fucking her blonde companion and was now standing over her face, insisting that the cock be licked clean. The woman, prone on the bench, did it gladly, savoring the taste of her own cunt on the huge rubber piece over her mouth. The crowd went wild as she sucked it—slowly—into her mouth until only the very root was visible, stuck into the harness low on the brunette's hips.

Cherry came to the corner of the bar and waited. Once she was satisfied, she never bothered to watch the remainder of the floor show. She had what she wanted.

"The usual for table four?" Slash called.

"Doubles this time," Cherry said. "I think your floor show got to them."

Slash smiled. "And it didn't get to you?" Cherry leaned over the bar and kissed the ruby lips that waited for her. "Only a warm-up. Are you and Ramone busy after closing? I think I'd like to show you a few tricks I learned on a piano bench myself."

Chapter Three

"My name is Mistress Angelina," the haughty black woman said.

Stef had already introduced herself. After the show was over, after the husky blonde had licked the huge rubber cock dry and had herself been thoroughly eaten by a submissive ordered onto the dance floor to do so, Stef had taken advantage of her midevening break. The dominatrix and submissive she had seen earlier had intrigued her, and when she went over to the table, the Mistress invited her to join them.

"And the slave?" Stef asked.

"Of no consequence," Angelina replied, without even looking over at the small, long-haired woman, who stared obediently at the tabletop in front of her. "Its name is Melissa, should you wish to command it."

Stef longed to. She had fierce dominant tendencies,

and she loved nothing more than to order a submissive around, with the spankings and cruelty that resulted when orders were not followed exactly. She had had her own submissives in the past, but once she started working at Rough Trade, she decided that it wasn't worth the trouble. Rather than commit herself to one or two submissives, and the time and effort required to keep them in line all the time, she simply got her fill from the clientele at the bar. Sometimes submissives would come in on their own, and Stef would pounce on them. But she preferred situations like this, where a Mistress was more than happy to share. This one seemed as if she wanted to, and Stef had jumped at the chance.

Stef ordered drinks for them. Angelina asked for an ice-cold martini, which had caused Ramone to shake her head silently when Cherry gave the order to her. Mistresses were always their toughest customers. They would ask for special drinks, insisting that they be made just so, and Ramone had remade hundreds of martinis that weren't precisely dry or sweet enough for these women. Ramone didn't always mind, though. Sometimes the dominatrixes would send their submissives to rectify the problem, and Ramone would always argue with them over it. It gave her great pleasure to see the horror in their eyes when they thought that they would not be able to carry out their Mistress's command of obtaining a properly mixed cocktail to take back to the table.

Angelina also ordered a glass of beer for Melissa, which surprised Stef; Mistresses usually didn't do this. Angelina saw her expression and explained, "She hasn't been allowed to drink anything all day." Stef smiled just as coldly as Angelina did. This was a submissive who was going to suffer.

When the beer arrived, given not to Melissa but put before Mistress Angelina—the waitresses in Rough Trade knew all the idiosyncrasies involved in serving dominatrixes and submissives—the black woman set it before her slave. Stef could see the wanting in her eyes, the almost-painful expression, and she could see Melissa swallow hard. She was terribly thirsty. But when she looked at Angelina with pleading eyes, she was ignored, and then Stef understood the seemingly benevolent and out-of-character act of ordering for the slave. The beer, cold and frosty, drops of moisture running down the sides of the glass, would sit there before the slave, taunting her, teasing her. The young woman would simply not be allowed to drink it.

"You have trained her very well," Stef said as she sipped her drink. She did not feel the least bit sorry for the woman, who sat greedily eyeing the beer; instead, she could feel her cunt warming up at the thought of torturing this creature further.

"Thank you," Angelina said as she sipped at her icy martini. "Of course you realize I would not have anything less."

"Of course." Stef played with the stem of her glass, while her attention was drawn to the dance floor.

The pounding music that Kiki played was too much for two of the women. They were dancing sensually, rubbing up and down against each other as they moved. Their mouths met and they pushed their tongues into each other as hard as they could. Stef watched as their hands moved to rub at pussies that must have been soaked under their jeans.

Completely unembarrassed, they shed their clothes effortlessly, so smoothly that the women dancing beside them never even noticed that they were now nude.

Glowing with sweat, they rubbed against each other and ran their hands over each other's nipples and thighs. Stef was fascinated by them, and out of the corner of her eye, she noticed that Mistress Angelina was watching them intently, too.

Not having been given permission to watch, Melissa sat miserably. Her gaze never left the icy beer in front of her, and Stef noticed that she had tears in her eyes. Rather than feel sorry for her, Stef had to overcome an almost overwhelming desire to slap the small woman across the face for the simple joy of watching her hand-print come up red on the pale skin.

Still dancing together, the two women slipped to their knees. In a moment, they were on the floor. They were so involved in each other they never noticed the hardness of the floor or the grittiness from so many shoes and boots. On their sides, head to feet, their mouths found each other's pussies automatically. Their tongues were blurs as they pushed into each other's cunts, groaning loudly and trying to get as deep inside as they could.

A couple beside them was too excited to ignore it. Within moments, they were naked and on the floor, too. Both of them moved in as easily as if cutting in on a dance. Stef stiffened, wondering if this would turn into a fight, if the newcomers would be rejected. But the two women were more interested in sex itself than each other, and the fact that these were new pussies they were licking didn't matter at all so long as they had a cunt to lick and a tongue deep in their own sticky grooves. The four quickly formed a daisy chain on the floor, all four of them grinding pussies into mouths, hands reaching to dip into soaked holes, pushing heads into their cunts as hard as they could, sticking their tongues into cuntfolds and flashing over clits.

It was automatic now that others would join them, and soon there were clothes spread all across the dance floor as naked women, all shapes, all sizes, all colors became overwhelmed by the need to lick and be licked, to give sex and get it in return.

The scene on the dance floor was rapidly turning into a free-for-all lickfest. As if it were a barroom brawl, women were noticing and then joining in as quickly as they could. The pair who had started it all were now on the bottom of a pile of writhing, sweaty, naked bodies. Mouths were licking whatever cunt was nearby; hands were reaching for tits and clits. Above it all, the music kept pounding while the colored lights flashed over everything.

It was obviously turning Angelina on, for she reached for Stef's hand and brought it between her legs. Stef reacted immediately, reaching up under Angelina's short leather skirt. There was nothing under it, and Stef's fingers quickly became soaked with pussyjuice. She heard Angelina moan softly as she brushed against the clit that was rockhard and wanting.

Stef could see that, at their place behind the bar, Ramone and Slash were at each other, hands and mouths moving over flesh. What she couldn't see was that behind the cover of the mahogany bar, they were standing with their legs wide open, and two lucky dykes who had been ordered to the floor were obediently lapping at their cunts for all they were worth.

"You want me, don't you?" Angelina murmured. "You want to discipline the slave also, don't you?"

"I would like that," Stef said as she massaged the hard, growing treat deep in the folds of Angelina's sopping pussy.

"Then why are we still out here?"

Women who had never visited the bar before, and who were staring wide-eyed and openmouthed at the orgy on the dance floor, wondered aloud how Stef and Angelina could just stand up and walk away. They didn't realize, as Stef did, that such a display was almost routine. Such a scene was played out fairly regularly on Rough Trade's floor, as women let themselves get carried away by the overwhelming sexual nature of the bar even as they danced before hundreds of others. There would be many more nights to stay and watch.

As she carried her drink and walked through the crowd, Stef smiled as she noticed Cherry coming up behind one of the wide-eyed neophytes. There was no doubt in her mind that the redheaded waitress would once again earn her nickname this evening.

Mistress Angelina followed Stef, with Melissa several steps behind. As ordered, she carried her glass of beer as she walked, and her eyes seldom left it. She was horribly thirsty; her tongue felt twice its normal size. She wanted that beer as much as anything she could imagine—she could feel it in her mouth, could taste it, knew how good it would be going down her parched throat.

But, more than anything, she wanted to please her Mistress Angelina, the woman she had to obey. Every muscle in her body obeyed her Mistress; every thought included her. She would not have touched the glass to her lips for anything, even if she did say a silent prayer in the hopes that Mistress Angelina would show some compassion and allow her a drink.

They walked through the bar, Angelina wearing her short leather skirt and an expensive cropped angora sweater, which showed off her firm tits and the nipples that poked at the fabric. She acknowledged admiring glances, both from women interested in the lusciousness of her body, and from other Mistresses who watched the way that Melissa followed so silently and obediently. It is no small thing to train a raw submissive, and it was obvious that Angelina had done so to perfection.

One of the two specially furnished rooms was busy, so Stef opened the door to the second one, which was slightly larger. The sight of the heavy table and the rings in the wall never failed to get her pussy churning with heat and want. This bigger room also had a large, over-stuffed recliner chair in one corner.

As the small woman walked through the door, her eyes properly downcast, Angelina took the glass from Melissa and ordered her to kneel. The girl did so, immediately, as Stef closed the door behind her.

"You poor little thing—you're so thirsty, aren't you?" she asked.

"Yes, Mistress," the small slave whispered.

"Then," Angelina said, "you shall have a drink."

She held the icy glass up to Stef and smiled. Stef looked at her, returning her smile, and dipped two fingers into the bitter liquid. Then she bent down to the small woman kneeling on the floor.

Melissa had her mouth open, waiting patiently for the drink. Her lips were dry and cracked, and Stef took great delight in moistening her lips slowly with the few drops of beer that clung to her fingers. When she straightened up, Angelina put the glass carefully on the far corner of the table.

Melissa seemed about to cry. The alcohol stung her parched lips. Her throat tightened when she realized that this was all she was going to get. Still, completely trained, she whispered, "Thank you, Mistress."

Now Angelina put the leather purse she had carried on the table. "Strip!" she ordered.

"Yes, Mistress," Melissa replied and unbuttoned her blouse.

Under the shirt, she was well built, with small breasts, one of which had a small steel ring through a hole in the nipple. "I put that there," Angelina said. "It comes in handy more often than you would believe."

The blouse had long sleeves. When she took it off, Melissa revealed that she was wearing thin leather straps around both wrists. A steel ring was set into each one. It was obvious that she was not going to receive permission to stand, and she wriggled out of her pants with great difficulty. Similar leather straps had been bound around her ankles.

It was not the straps that held Stef's attention, though, but Melissa's body. She was mottled with bruises in several places, and Stef looked her over carefully, studying them. A rash of them across her back, some of them long and thin, could have come only from a whip's being brought down over and over on the skin. Bruises on her thighs could have been caused by a paddle, or a hairbrush. Two bruises circling her upper arms looked like straps pulled so tightly they cut into the flesh. Most exciting, though, was the dark area on her tit, right around the steel ring set into the nipple.

Angelina had been finishing her martini while Stef examined the small woman's body. "Now," she said, "you're probably wondering about that tit. Nicely done, isn't it? I'll show you how useful these things can be."

She reached down. Melissa, who knew from experience what was about to happen, closed her eyes and sucked in her breath, but did not move. Angelina put one index finger through the steel ring in her nipple. Then she lifted it.

Melissa had to keep from screaming as she struggled

to rise, dragged by the ring in her breast. The bruised skin of her tit was pulled tight as the ring held solid in the flesh of her nipple. Angelina's eyes were bright as she watched her slave try to avoid crying out. Stef's cunt was now so hot she thought she could feel its juice on her thigh. This woman was totally cruel, and Stef loved it.

In a movement so fast and smooth that Stef barely saw it, Angelina let go of the ring and smashed Melissa from behind. The little slave fell hard, chest first, onto the top of the heavy table. She was gasping for breath, but she didn't move. Her feet were still on the floor and she was bent at the waist, her luscious little bare ass sticking out for the two dominatrixes to admire.

From her bag, Angelina extracted two chains, which she hooked to the rings on Melissa's wrist straps. She then chained her to the table, one arm to each table leg, so that the submissive was spread across the top of it, her back vulnerable.

"She would not move a muscle unless I gave her permission," Angelina explained. "But I simply can't resist the sight of a woman shackled down."

"I can't either," Stef admitted, and she moved behind Angelina to get a better look at the slave. As she did, she put her arms around the tall black woman and felt the perfect breasts through the soft, silky sweater.

Angelina leaned back, into Stef, enjoying the feeling of a fellow dominatrix's fingers on her tits. She turned and the two met in a long kiss, with Stef's hands moving under the sweater to touch the smooth skin and the hard, bumpy nipples. Angelina, in turn, had her hands on Stef's ass, massaging her buttocks through Stef's thin pants.

Stef slipped out of them at once, and Angelina did the same, dropping the leather skirt but retaining the black leather boots that she wore. Melissa, facing away from them, could see none of it, and she wanted to sob. Her beloved Mistress receiving pleasure from another woman! It was always the bane of a slave's existence when it was not her lips and tongue eliciting pleasure from her Mistress's cunt.

"Perhaps," Angelina whispered, sighing as Stef reached for the ruby folds of her cunt, "we can have a bit of fun with this slave, and then a bit of fun with each other."

She reached into the bag, which obviously contained an entire assortment of playthings, and pulled out a leather-faced paddle. "Would you like to try it out?" she asked.

She moved to the other side of the table to take pleasure in Melissa's scarlet cheeks. The small young slave was mortified. Not only was this stranger pleasuring her Mistress, but now she would be taking the liberty of administering punishment!

Stef hefted the paddle in her hand, admiring its weight. It was a serious tool, a carved hickory handle topped with a thick, flat pad of black leather. When she smacked it lightly into her hand, she could feel the sting. A harsh blow must be a horrible punishment.

Then she looked carefully at Melissa's buttocks. They were firm, tight, the skin rich and creamy over them, pale and delicate. It would show up the blow from a paddle very well. She aimed for what she felt would give her the maximum angle.

Thwack! Both of the dominatrixes smiled as the paddle came down. Melissa grunted and her body trembled. As she expected, Stef watched as the skin turned deathly white for just a second, and then welled up bright red as the blood rushed to the injury. It was a delicious sight.

From her post at the front of the table, Angelina enjoyed the sight of her small slave's expression. It was a strange yet completely satisfying mixture of pain, terror, shame and, curiously, a deep-seated pleasure that only such punishment could produce in her.

Stef was becoming more excited with each blow. She staggered them, one gratifying smack on each buttock. They welled up a brilliant red with each blow, then settled into a delicious mottled burgundy just under the skin. Stef stopped to admire her handiwork, and Melissa let out her breath in a sigh of relief, thinking her punishment was finished. That was premature; the leather paddle smacked down again.

Melissa was determined she was not going to cry for this stranger. Only her beloved Mistress could make her do that!

"She holds back very well," Stef observed. She knew that Melissa wanted to sob, wanted to scream with the burning that started at her asscheeks and went through her whole shackled body, but that she bit her swollen lip for pride.

"She always does," Angelina replied. "She fashions herself to be such a brave little fool."

Stef smacked again, this time on the tops of her thighs, and Melissa gasped. This was a much more tender area than her buttocks, and she choked back her tears. "They're all fools," Stef said. "That's why they're chained at our feet."

She worked this area hard. The room was close with the sound of the paddle on submissive skin, with the rich aroma of leather and needy pussies, and the film of sweat that covered Melissa's body.

Finally Melissa could take no more. With a sob that racked her entire body, she burst into tears. "Mercy,

Mistress!" she screamed. "Please, mercy! Mistress Angelina, please, please make her stop!"

The two dominatrixes smiled at each other over the prone body of the whimpering submissive. "Is there any sweeter sound than that?" Angelina asked.

"I don't believe so," Stef replied. She handed the paddle over the table to Angelina. The black woman held it before her captive slave's face. Without any verbal commands, Melissa kissed the paddle and thanked it for the punishment she had received. Her training was so thorough that no command was needed; she was expected to give thanks to every device that wreaked cruel torture upon her body. She continued to sob, though, for she had taken an incredible amount of abuse.

"Too much of anything is not good, even a submissive's screams," Angelina said, and she opened the purse again. This time she took out two large cotton handkerchiefs, snowy white and freshly starched. One of them she balled up; placing her thumb hard on Melissa's lower lip, she forced her mouth open, then crammed the wadded handkerchief inside. Melissa swallowed hard several times, fighting nausea, fighting the choking sensation. The second handkerchief was twisted into a rope, strung through Melissa's mouth, and then tied behind her head as an effective way of keeping the gag inside. Stef watched with pleasure. She loved to see knots and restraints used on a helpless slave.

Also from the purse came a long, thin chrome chain with a tiny snap at one end. Angelina smacked Melissa hard, until the little submissive arched her back as best she could to lift her chest off the table. Of course, it wasn't far enough for Angelina, who smacked the girl again. Then she reached under Melissa's body and snapped the chain onto the steel ring that went through one nipple, and fed the chain out like fishing line across the floor.

Turned on more than she could imagine by the scene, Angelina was on the other side of the table in a moment. They ignored the tears and muffled, choking sobs as they met, their arms wrapped around each other, their mouths open and searching for the tongues that were thrust inside.

They made their way to the reclining chair; Stef got in it first and lay almost flat. Angelina turned around, the musky leather of her boots like a perfume to Stef, and lowered herself over the woman who waited so eagerly beneath her.

Stef could never resist chocolate-colored flesh, and she dove in heartily. Angelina's cunt seemed as sweet as chocolate, too, and so soaked with her own thick fluid that it gleamed hot on the inside of her thighs. She could hear Melissa sob again, this time with frustration, knowing that her Mistress's orgasm would be courtesy of another dominatrix, and not her own tongue.

Angelina was into the sixty-nine just as quickly. Like most Mistresses, she insisted on nothing but the best, and provided exactly the same. Her tongue was liquid fire in Stef's cunt. Stef felt a warmth go through her whole body as Angelina pointed her tongue and then stuffed it as far as she could into Stef's velvety hole.

Stef responded by pushing aside the dark folds of skin with her tongue. Angelina's pussy was an oyster, moist and salty, and she felt the woman over her groan with delight when the tip of her tongue found the smooth, hard pearl at the top of it. Deftly, she slipped first one finger and then a second into the wet tunnel. She loved the way the velvety walls held her fingers in a muscular grip, and she pulled out and pushed in, fucking Angelina with her hand.

By this time, Melissa had quieted down, which was not good enough for the two bloodthirsty dominatrixes. Stef had all but forgotten the thin chrome chain, but Angelina had not. She reached for the end of it with a free hand and pulled.

Only the handkerchief in Melissa's mouth kept her from screaming at the top of her lungs. As it was, her agony came out as a choked, muffled cry as the chain pulled hard and stretched the nipple with its cruel restraint. Angelina never missed a beat of the rhythm she kept up on Stef's cunt, and when Melissa calmed down again, it took only a single sharp tug of the chain to send her reeling once more. Swallowing hard to fight down the sickening feeling, Melissa thought she was going to choke on the starched handkerchief. Her face was bright red, and her cheeks were soaked with tears.

Stef and Angelina were soaked also, but with a sweeter liquid, one that they both lapped up greedily from each other's cunts. The sound of their licking was horrid to Melissa's ears—that was her Mistress's cunt! That was the cunt she lived to pleasure! All in one breath she hated, feared, and yet admired Mistress Stef. Against everything else, she longed for a chance to please her also.

They continued for a long time. They built each other up, lapping hard, then held back to tease each other. Whenever Melissa became quiet again, Angelina tugged on the chain. The muffled screams sent a rush through them, and they stepped up their licking.

Angelina came first. She was very vocal, and her cries of pleasure started Melissa sobbing again. Never did her Mistress cry out when the tongue between her legs was that of a submissive! When Melissa pleasured her Mistress, the only indication of an orgasm was a slight shiver and then a cuff to the ears to knock the slave away. No matter how well Melissa might perform, no matter how nicely her tongue would dance on Mistress Angelina's clit, the sweet screams of her pleasure was a sound Melissa would never be able to produce.

The black woman rode it out, grinding on Stef's face, but her mouth stayed on Stef's cunt. Stef couldn't hold out, and a hard sucking on her clit, along with a scream from Melissa when her chain was tugged, was enough to send her over the edge. She let the tide of chilled heat wash over her, right out to the ends of her fingers, and she groaned and gasped with its intensity.

When they both calmed down enough, they climbed out of the chair. "So you like my little toy?" Angelina asked as she ran the thin chain between her fingers.

"I've never seen anything like that before," Stef admitted. "Chains with weights, yes, or chaining them to the wall. But I never thought of keeping them screaming while I'm busy with someone else. I like that."

"You have to keep them on their toes," Angelina explained as she untied the handkerchief that kept the gag in Melissa's mouth. "I like to hear them scream." She pulled the wet, wadded handkerchief out of the young woman's mouth.

Thirsty before, Melissa was now almost crazy for a drink, and Angelina noticed her staring at the glass of beer. It was still on the table in front of her, still cool enough to leave drops of moisture on the glass. "The starch in the handkerchief certainly leaves your mouth dry, doesn't it?" Angelina asked.

"Yes, Mistress." It was a parched whisper.

"And this beer looks nice and cold, doesn't it? So cold, so wet, I'll bet it would go down as smooth as silk," the black woman continued.

"Yes, Mistress." It was a sob.

"Then," Angelina said, "I'll test it to be sure."

Melissa's tear-filled eyes never blinked as she watched her Mistress take a long drink out of the glass. She passed it to Stef, who touched the side of the cold glass to Melissa's hot forehead before she took a drink herself. The Mistresses continued to pass it back and forth, each one taunting a bit more by waving it in front of the chained slave or placing a drop on her lips. When it was empty, Angelina set it down on the table.

"A very satisfying evening," she said to Stef.

"I have to go back to work," Stef said. "I would like to thank you for the use of your submissive, and for..." There was no need to finish with words; a deep kiss did that. Then she dressed and opened the door.

Angelina remained naked, except for the leather boots. As Stef stood in the doorway, she watched the tall black woman reach into the purse and bring out a hairbrush, the heavy, wooden-handled kind that could be used for so much more than grooming hair.

The screams could be heard even as Stef closed the door behind her. She looked at her watch. Her next break was in two hours; perhaps they would still be in the room by then.

Chapter Four

Cherry looked on as Stef led the way from the tightly packed crowd watching the orgy on the dance floor, followed by the elegant black woman and, some steps later, by the downcast submissive. She wished her friend well for the evening, as they all did for each other whenever they found someone from the crowd to add interest to the night.

Cherry knew Stef's love of domination well. She had often joined in when Stef had honed in on a single, unaccompanied submissive out for a night on her own. For a moment, she considered asking to join in, but decided against it. She wasn't really in the mood to dominate this evening. She had her own specialty, and tonight seemed like the perfect night to indulge in it.

Like a panther on the prowl, she watched the women who were mesmerized by the scene on the dance floor.

Although obviously turned on and fascinated by the women licking each other on the floor, many of them were regulars and they treated it as just another normal occurrence at Rough Trade. Cherry recognized many of them; they came in night after night.

Many more were just turned on, and some were obviously debating getting out of their clothes and joining in. But there were a very few who were completely different from all the others, and these were the ones Cherry focused on.

They were wide-eyed, and their mouths were open in surprise or even outright shock. It was obvious they had never seen such a sight before. Certainly, they were never expecting to see it right in front of their eyes, live, real, on the floor of a bar. They were amazed, overwhelmed, a little frightened, but through it all Cherry could see that they were excited. She spotted them immediately. They were virgins.

She narrowed them down to three as they stood in the crowd, gaping at the scene. One looked too shocked; she might flee like a frightened deer. Another already had a woman standing beside her, talking to her; Cherry made it a rule never to get in the way of a woman hitting on another, even if it was a luscious virgin, and besides, there was another choice. It was the third woman who caught her eye.

She was lovely, her blonde hair cut short, her lips full and pursed as she watched. Her tits were a nice size and her hips were full, nicely proportioned. Cherry loved women like that; she loved to hang on to those hips, one on each side, and bury her face in the hot mound that was waiting for her below. She liked the look of this woman, so she worked her way through the crowd until she was standing right beside her.

The woman's perfume was dazzling, and Cherry breathed it in deeply. Her pussy was throbbing; she longed to reach between her legs to massage it. Of course she didn't. This was all part of her plan. The buildup, the longing, the aching that seemed to go on for an eternity was part of what made taking a virgin so exciting for her. The sexual tension made her tingle as if an electric current was flowing through her body. If it took all night, it only added to the pleasure.

Cherry sized up the woman, thrilled by the look of unabashed shock and excitement on her face. Motioning nonchalantly to the women on the floor, she said, "Isn't that something?"

The blonde woman turned quickly, startled, and saw that Cherry was speaking to her. She turned red. Standing in a room filled to capacity with women, she was somehow embarrassed that Cherry had seen her watching. "Yes...yes, it is," she said, and then turned away. She looked back to the scene on the floor, but now nervously, mortified that Cherry's attention was on her while she watched.

Cherry certainly hadn't earned her name by giving up easily. "You've never been in here before, have you?" she asked.

Again the quick look, the swift reddening of the cheeks, which made Cherry want her all the more. "No, no," she said. "Never."

Cherry moved closer, on an angle to the dance floor. It was now difficult for the blonde woman to turn away from her without also turning her back on the writhing orgy of bodies on the dance floor. "Are you here by yourself?"

The blonde was paying a bit more attention to Cherry now. "Yes," she said. "My girlfriend was supposed to come with me, but she couldn't. I came by myself." It was spoken quickly, almost rehearsed, and Cherry had to suppress a smile. How alike they all were! If only they knew, as they tried so hard to blend in, that they stuck out as much as if they stood there wearing neon clothes and flashing lights. Virgins! How Cherry loved them!

Most of the tables near the dance floor were empty; the women sitting at them had risen and moved away to get a better view of the scene. "They'll be there for a long time." Cherry indicated the women who were moaning, thrashing about, pushing their tongues into any cunts close to them, grabbing any tits they could. "Come over here and let me buy you a drink. White wine okay?"

She reached up to call for drinks, but there was no need. They were on their way. Watching from the bar, Slash had noticed Cherry hitting on the well-built blonde and had set up two glasses with the order Cherry always placed under the circumstances. The blonde was a bit surprised when the glass appeared almost instantly, but didn't say anything about it.

"How rude of me," Cherry said as she reached for her drink. "I never introduced myself; my name is Cherry."

"That's an interesting name," the woman said. Her name was Nora, and when Cherry lifted her glass in a toast, she held up her own shyly and let Cherry reach over to touch the goblets together with a tiny clink.

"To a most interesting evening," Cherry said.

Nora looked out at the dance floor. "It certainly is," she said.

Cherry's pussy was throbbing, and when she looked over, she noticed that Nora's nipples were hard and pointed, pushing at the fabric of her shirt. Ever so slowly, she reached over and placed her hand lightly on Nora's leg, just above her knee.

She could feel the muscles tighten under her fingers, but she didn't pull her hand away. Instead, she acted as calmly as she could, and sipped her wine.

Nora's face was bright red. "Does it bother you?" Cherry asked.

"No," Nora said. "Only...well, I've never done anything like this before."

Cherry moved her hand an inch up Nora's thigh. "I'm sure you didn't come in here because you were thirsty," she said.

Nora couldn't help smiling nervously. "I've always been curious," she said. "I lied about my friend coming with me. I heard some women at the office talking about this place, so I came by myself. I wanted to see if what they said was true."

"It is, isn't it?"

"More than I thought," Nora said. "I like to watch movies of women together, I like to read about them. I never thought I'd ever see something like this." She looked to the dance floor, where it seemed as if half the crowd was naked and fucking each other wherever they could.

"But you've never had a woman, have you?" Cherry asked. She had pulled her chair closer.

"No," Nora admitted.

Cherry leaned forward. "It's even better than the movies." And boldly, she kissed Nora's lips.

The blonde woman gasped as she did, and she trembled a little, but she did not move back from the red-haired woman who had taken such a liberty. As Cherry kissed her again, this time moving her hand up to the middle of Nora's thigh, she felt Nora lean into her. To her delight, the third kiss was returned.

Now Cherry became even bolder. The music was pounding around them. Sounds of groaning and gasping could be heard from the dance floor. She touched her tongue to Nora's lips. There was only a slight hesitation, and then Nora opened her mouth to accept it. In a moment, her own tongue rose to meet Cherry's, cautiously and then with more enthusiasm. Cherry was sure that if she were to put her hand between Nora's legs, her fingers would come away hot and wet.

For all her newfound excitement, Nora's hands were still on the table, her fingers around the stem of her wineglass. Cherry kissed her throat, never stumbling at all even as she unbuttoned her own shirt, so smoothly that Nora didn't even know it was open. She took Nora's hand and guided it between the rows of buttons, to the breast underneath.

Nora gasped and looked around, but Cherry was still kissing her neck, her voice low and reassuring in Nora's ear. "Look at the dance floor," she said. "Do you think anyone cares what you're doing over here? No one's even watching." The touch on her nipple was soft and unsure, and Cherry almost came right there. She loved their uncertainty and raw naïveté.

Nora couldn't see the dragon tattoo, but she stopped instantly when she came to the gold ring in Cherry's nipple. "Oh…" she began, but her fingers didn't leave the spot. "That's interesting." She felt the ring all over, and Cherry shivered as a hot flush went from her nipple right through her whole body. It seemed to carve a feverish path through her body right down to her cunt, where it waited, throbbing, begging for sexual relief.

"Is your pussy hot?" Cherry asked.

"It's—yes—I've never done this before," Nora said. "I've never felt like this, ever."

Cherry was still nuzzling at Nora's throat, kissing her earlobes, the strong line of her jaw. "You can stay a virgin all your life and wonder what it might have been like," she said. "Or I have somewhere we can go."

Still shy, still disbelieving, still sure she would wake up and find it was all a delicious dream, Nora could only nod in silence. Cherry picked up both the wineglasses and stood up. "Follow me," she said. When Nora looked at her, Cherry assured her, "It's a place where we can have some privacy. Don't worry, you have nothing to be afraid of. We're not going to leave the bar, and I would never do anything to hurt you. All I give is pleasure."

The original pair of women who started everything out on the dance floor were now off to the side, satisfied and sitting together, admiring what they had started. The knot of women on the floor was just as hot as ever, and there seemed to be no end in sight. Whenever one or more women left the orgy, more would come in to take their place. Cherry looked up at Slash and winked at her. The beautiful black woman behind the bar simply shook her head good-naturedly; it was unbelievable how many virgins Cherry could convince to follow her to the back rooms.

Reality hit Nora when she saw the room with the cot in it; up until then, it had only been kisses and whispered promises. She stopped in the doorway, suddenly shy and unsure. Cherry squeezed her own thighs together hard. The pressure on her clit was delicious. Every one of them always stopped right here, always held back at the doorway. Virgins were so delightful!

She worked her way into Nora's arms again. "The best is yet to come." And she kissed the full lips. The first two kisses were not returned, but as Nora relaxed in her arms, it became mutual again.

"I'm nervous," Nora admitted. "I've never done this before."

"I think you've already told me that," Cherry smiled. "There was a time you never tried champagne or chocolate, either," she added. Before Nora even knew what was happening, Cherry had guided her into the room expertly and closed the door.

The muffled sounds of the bar behind them, the two women stood in the small, half-lit room and kissed. Cherry's hands were now making their way down Nora's body. Her breasts felt lovely and heavy in Cherry's hands, and Cherry could feel Nora tighten and then tremble as Cherry's fingers found the nipples. Cherry knew the heat that was going through the blonde's body; it was coursing through her own right now.

Cherry was an expert. Nora knew that her shirt was open only when she felt the air on her skin. She was right into this now, though, and her embarrassment was not only nonexistent, but she could hardly wait to be completely naked in front of this stranger. When she reached behind her back to unhook her own bra, Cherry's cunt radiated heat through her body to the tips of her fingers.

She was beautiful naked. Her hair was naturally blonde; her pussyhair was long, silky, and golden. Cherry took off her own shirt, and Nora was fascinated by the colorful dragon that wove its way around her shoulder and finished at the gold ring in the nipple.

Cherry laid her down on the cot. "When it's your first time, it should be extra-special," she said. "You don't have to do anything. Just sit back and enjoy."

Nora looked magnificent lying on the cot, with her tits pointing up and her mound glowing gold in the half-light of the room. She was a piece of candy, and Cherry didn't know which end to start at. Finally she started at Nora's feet, so that she could look up and watch the woman she was deflowering.

She started by massaging Nora's feet, running her hands along the smooth skin of her legs. Nora almost purred at this attention, and she stretched out on the cot. Cherry spent a long time just running her fingers over the skin and planting tiny kisses. When she gently parted Nora's thighs a couple of inches, she was happy to see that the pussyhair gleamed with wetness.

When she got to Nora's thighs she teased the sensitive skin on the inside for the longest time. She was thrilled to hear Nora gasp and then groan. "Anything wrong?" Cherry asked innocently, with a mischievous smile.

The woman on the cot was unsure of herself, but in a different way this time. "There's a throbbing between my legs," she said. "It's so hot, I can't believe it. Why is it doing this?"

It was Cherry's turn to be surprised. "Well, it's telling you it wants to come, honey," she said. "What did you think it was?"

Nora was squirming on the cot. "I didn't know. It's never been like this."

Cherry stopped and looked at her. "What, doesn't it always throb and go hot just before you come?"

Nora was almost overcome with a mixture of embarrassment and self-pity. She caught her breath just before she sobbed. "I don't…I mean, I've never come before."

Cherry could only stare at her. "Never?"

"No." Nora looked at her. "I had a few boyfriends, but I guess they weren't into that. They just got on top and did their thing. I didn't even know it was supposed to be different until I read about it and realized I'd never had it happen. That's why I came here. I thought maybe having a woman would be different."

Although still surprised by the confession, Cherry

grinned at her. "You have no idea," she said. "A woman knows exactly how it feels, so she knows exactly how to make someone else feel that way."

Always determined that she should give a virgin the orgasm of her life, Cherry was now on a mission. Not only the best but the first! She felt like a savior as she ran her tongue along the creamy pale skin of Nora's thighs.

Nora was squirming on the cot now. "That feels so nice," she said. Her head was thrown back on the pillowless cot, her short hair bunched up, and Cherry thought she was exquisite with her eyes closed and her mouth half-opened. Cherry longed to put her own pussy on those full lips. She could only take so much tenderness, though, and even as she moved up Nora's thighs she was considering her next move. She had done it with others; she was sure it would work well with this one.

When she reached Nora's pussy, she blew gently on the hairs. Nora groaned at the warmth. Cherry followed it up by running the very tip of her tongue over the ends of Nora's blonde pussyhairs. Without even touching the skin, she sent rivers of liquid heat through Nora's entire body.

Nora cried out at the first long lap of Cherry's tongue through the thick, sweet folds of her cunt. Her cry turned to a long, low guttural moan as Cherry pushed into her pussy to find the hot nub at the top of it.

"That's your clit," Cherry said as Nora looked down at her. "That's what we worship here."

"Then worship it," Nora said, and to add to Cherry's excitement, she reached down to touch her pleasure-giver's hair. Her fingers wove through the brilliant red strands and then, unable to control herself, she pulled

Cherry's head into her pussy. She wanted more, and she was determined to get it.

There was no more slow buildup. Cherry was now deep in Nora's pussy, and licking hard and fast over the clit. Her finger rimmed the entrance to Nora's hole and then, swiftly, entered the hot tunnel. It was wet with thick fluid. Cherry stopped to lick her finger dry, enjoying the salt-sweet taste, then returned to the clit when Nora groaned and pulled Cherry back in.

She could feel Nora's clit grow under her tongue, even as the woman groaned louder and bucked her hips up and down on the cot. The taste of her cunt became tangy, oyster-coppery. Then she began to come.

It built up with a heat that Nora could hardly imagine. It started deep in her belly, at the root of her clit, and spread throughout her entire body until she was trembling. She screamed her selfish pleasure, held Cherry's head into her cunt and ground it against her. Her muscles were as tight as ropes as she shivered, crying out. Finally the last wave broke and she fell back, exhausted.

Cherry stayed on the wet pussy and licked the hot fluid out of the swollen folds until everything was dry. Nora shivered again, hard, at the touch of the tongue on her sensitive flesh.

"Was it anything like what you read?" Cherry asked as she licked her lips to get every last drop of Nora's flavorful pussyjuice.

Nora lounged on the cot, every muscle in her body relaxed and satisfied. "Now I understand when they say they feel the earth move!" she gasped.

Cherry's pussy was throbbing, and she stroked it gently through her pants to take the edge off. "You will find it surprising to know that it only gets better from here," she said. She was starting to feel aggressive; the virgin had been deflowered gently, and now it was coming to Cherry's time to enjoy herself.

"Better?"

Cherry smiled, but now it was a cool one. "You want to eat my pussy, too, don't you?"

"Oh, yes!" The reply was immediate, and Cherry unbuttoned her pants slowly. "That was…that's what I always watched in the movies. It looked so good. I've always wanted to try it…. I really don't know much about it, though."

"Don't be stupid." Nora was surprised at the cold, harsh tinge in Cherry's voice. "You didn't know about orgasms, and you enjoyed that one, didn't you? You know what feels good. You just do it to me. It will come automatically to you."

The next few moments blurred by so quickly that Nora was never really sure what happened. In a flash, Cherry's strong hand was around her wrist, pulling her up. The door was opening, and the blonde virgin was being thrust outside, into the thick of the crowd.

Nora screamed and tried to draw back, but Cherry was too powerful. "You got yours your way," she said. "Now I get mine the way I want it!"

Nora's screams turned to wretched sobs as she was pulled through the crowd, toward the dance floor. She cried for someone to help her, but there was no chance. All of the women in the crowd were waiting, craning their necks, eager to see what was going to happen. Behind the bar, Slash watched patiently. She had seen this scene carried out so many times, but each time it was like the first; and despite the many orgasms she had had that day, her pussy juiced up again with anticipation.

The dance floor was almost empty; only a few women

were still down, licking and caressing each other. The piano bench was still there, and Nora was pushed down on it, on her back. She tried to get up but could not. Before she could, Cherry was completely naked, her pussy straddled over Nora's face. There was nowhere for Nora to go.

"Lick it!" Cherry commanded. The crowd was back on its feet now, watching this fascinating twist in the evening's entertainment.

"I can't—they're watching!" Nora sobbed.

Cherry lowered herself so that Nora's mouth was completely covered by her pussy. It was the perfect gag, hot and wet, waiting. Nora couldn't say anything because her mouth was filled with it. "Lick it!" Cherry ordered. "You came here for this, didn't you? You told me you wanted it. Now you've got it! Lick it or I'll push it down your throat!"

Her mouth filled with pussy, her throat choked with sobs, Nora almost involuntarily thrust out her tongue. Cherry groaned at the first touch of it on her clit, and she rubbed her cunt over Nora's mouth. Nora kept her tongue out and Cherry moved the groove of her pussy over it. On the second pass, she was delighted to find, Nora was actually licking it on her own. When Nora's tongue found the twin rings in her cuntlips, Cherry went wild.

"It's nice, isn't it?" Cherry said as she felt Nora reaching up to her clit. Her groping was clumsy, but the excitement made up for it.

"Yes, oh, yes!" Nora cried. "Yes—oooh!" Cherry looked down and smiled. Another woman had come out of the crowd, unable to resist the temptation of Nora's open legs, and her mouth was now tight on the blonde pussy, her tongue working its way into the crack.

Within moments the sobbing, frightened virgin was transformed. It was so unbelievable to her that she felt she was watching someone else instead of doing it herself. She couldn't get enough of Cherry's cunt and, to her surprise, the knowledge that the whole room was watching her naked, eating another woman, being sucked herself, was turning her on. She dug her fingers into Cherry's asscheeks to pull them down closer to her. She wished she could crawl right into Cherry's hole and fuck her from the inside out.

Cherry bounced on her, pushed her cunt in closer even as she held her tits up and massaged her own nipples. The crowd cried out its approval and when she came, groaning her pleasure, the women watching roared with her. When she got off and kissed Nora as deeply as she could, the room seemed to spin.

"Your clothes are back in the room," Cherry told her. "But I don't think you'll want them for a while yet." She could see that several women in the crowd were eyeing the naked blonde and she knew that soon, there would be another group of women on the floor fucking each other. Nora noticed them also and to her surprise she could hardly wait for them. Cherry smiled at her, and then began to look the crowd over, searching for the faces that showed a mixture of shock and surprise, the look of women who were virgins.

Behind the bar, Slash poured another beer and called over one of the waitresses. "Tell Cherry to come over and see me when she's free."

"You got a job for her?" Ramone asked as she dried a glass.

Slash looked out at the crowd, at the blonde woman lying naked on the bench. Another woman had come up and had positioned herself between Nora's legs, while two others were massaging her tits, taking the nipples between their teeth. It looked as if a fourth woman was going to straddle Nora's mouth. Nora waited with her tongue out, hoping that someone would.

Slash looked at Cherry, putting her pants on and taking a long drink from a friend's glass of beer. "Let's just say," the tall woman said, "that I'd like a little taste of the dragon myself."

Chapter Five

"Come on in," Slash called. "Be careful you don't trip over it, you might fall."

Ramone walked into the huge loft, lit by the midmorning sun coming through the windows. She heeded Slash's warning and stepped aside to avoid the obstruction.

"It" was a young woman, naked, sitting on her buttocks on the hard floor. Her eyes were covered by a heavy black leather blindfold buckled behind her head. Also buckled in place was a large ball gag that distended her mouth and stretched her lips painfully, and a leather dog collar tight around her throat. Her long black hair was pulled into a tight braid.

A wide strap went around her torso and buckled tightly in front, but she could not have reached to open it even if she had wanted to. It held a black metal rod that ran up her spine and ended two feet above her head with a chrome ring. From this ring went two short chains, which were snapped to the straps around her wrists. Her arms were held up at the height of her naked breasts, which were adorned with nipple clips. Her ankles were strapped together and her knees were spread wide; a huge pink dildo was stuffed into her cunt.

Ramone whistled softly as she walked around the woman on the floor, admiring the handiwork. "Very nice," she said approvingly. "You've outdone yourself."

Slash came out of the bathroom. She was wearing a form-fitting suit, crafted in brilliant electric blue that shimmered in the light, and matching blue stiletto-heeled shoes. Around her waist was a black leather belt finished with a heavy chrome buckle. Ramone stopped for a moment to admire her; no matter what Slash wore, she always looked fabulous.

"Where did you find it?" Ramone asked, motioning to the bound woman. The young captive could not see her, but still trembled slightly at her words. Her arms were numb from being held up, and her jaw ached from the ball gag. Her pussy was distended with the huge cock and her nipples were on fire from the clamps. Her whole body throbbed painfully with the agony of being forced into one position for the hours she had stayed there. Yet despite all this—because of all this—she was happier than she had ever been. She was being allowed to serve Slash, and this, for her, was the highest honor imaginable.

"It was hanging around the bar last night," Slash said. "It didn't seem to want to leave, so I thought, what the hell, take it home."

"You're very generous." Ramone looked carefully at the young woman, who was hanging on every word.

"Too generous," Slash agreed. The women smiled at each other over the blindfolded captive's head. "But I figured if it didn't amuse me, I'd just leave it naked and put it out on the street." The young woman shivered again; she knew Slash's reputation and knew that such a nasty threat would be carried out with no qualms whatsoever. She could imagine herself out on the sidewalk, during the rush hour of New York's streets, completely naked, her body bearing the unmistakable bruises and marks of her servitude, trying to find a place to hide, to get back to her own home. Her breath bubbled past the ball gag as she drew a quaking gasp.

"So what do you have planned?" Ramone asked. Her voice was sultry; her look was wanting. Slash had called her, invited her to come over, and Ramone was ready for whatever Slash had in mind.

Slash smiled. "I was hungry," she said. "I thought I might like something special. I was thinking of sushi—warm and raw."

The woman on the floor was curious, but Ramone knew exactly what she was talking about. "We haven't had that for a long time," she agreed. "Now that you mention it, I could really go for that."

"Then what are we waiting for?" Slash motioned to the far end of the loft, where her bed was situated.

Ramone stayed where she was. "Can't we have a little fun first?" she asked.

"Of course," Slash said. "I'm sorry I never thought to ask. I'd like that, too."

With one quick movement of her blue stiletto shoes, she kicked the submissive over on her side. As she fell, the young woman's scream was clearly audible through the ball gag.

The slave almost passed out as she hit the floor hard.

Her hands stayed above her and she fell hard against her wrist as the chains clattered on the wooden floor. The metal clamps pulled on her nipples and sent horrid fire through her tits right through to her spine. Her knees took the brunt of the fall because she could not move her shackled ankles, and the dildo was shoved hard into her cunt. Slash was an expert; everything she had done to the young woman worked against her as she lay on her side, sobbing into the ball gag, still unable to see her tormentor's cruel smile. Even crying was painful; the collar was loose enough when she was relaxed, but it tightened demonically when she gasped for breath.

"What's its name?" Ramone asked. The slave feared Slash, but she was even more unsure of the Japanese woman because she could not see her. She had no idea whether Ramone was wearing street clothes or the stylized costume of a dominatrix. She did not know if Ramone came with empty hands, or carried a whip or a paddle. For all she knew, Ramone might even be a submissive herself, ordered by a cruel Mistress to speak this way and confuse the bound woman even more. All of the uncertainty was working, though; Ramone could see that the submissive's pussylips, distended fully around the pink rubber dildo, were wet with the juice of sexual need.

"I didn't ask," Slash said. "I didn't care to know. I suppose we can call it anything we like. How about... oh, Dog will do, I guess. It *is* wearing a collar, after all."

"That'll do just fine," Ramone said, and the young woman, now known as Dog, tried to control both her tears and her trembling.

Slash unbuckled the leather belt from around her waist and held it up. She shook it, and the chrome buckle clanged in an unmistakable way that Dog identified immediately. She had been a submissive for many years and had served many Mistresses. By just the sound, she knew what style of buckle it was and— worse—its heft. The jangle gave it away as being a very heavy one.

"On your stomach!" Slash ordered. Dog tried to, but she could not, and she sobbed miserably when she realized she could not carry out this Mistress's command. The chains on her wrists, the pole against her spine, and the shackles on her ankles prevented her from doing anything but swaying ineffectively. She could not turn herself over.

"I don't think it's trying hard enough," Ramone observed.

"It isn't, is it?" Slash said, and both of them laughed at the sight of Dog stepping up her efforts in an attempt to prove wordlessly that she was doing her best. Desperate, she automatically tried to speak to them, to beg forgiveness for not carrying out the command. Slash and Ramone laughed again, this time at the words that the ball gag rendered incomprehensible.

"They are funny, aren't they?" Ramone said. Dog stiffened; it was the voice that usually preceded a stripe with the whip. Noticing this, Ramone stepped closer, making sure that her footsteps were audible on the bare floor. Dog trembled again, waiting for the blow. Ramone smiled. She loved to have them in such a state of uncertainty; she could punish them without even touching them.

She broke the uncertainty by reaching down and grabbing the slave by her long, thick braid. "Your Mistress gave you a command," she hissed. "The first thing a stupid cunt like you should learn is how to obey!"

The young woman, her eyes covered, her mouth distended and gagged, had no way to proclaim her innocence. Helplessly, she held up her open palms in the time-honored gesture of servitude and obedience. She suspected it would not work—she knew she was being set up—but it was the only chance she had. She held her breath to see. Ramone watched her, standing over her with her hand on the woman's hair. Then she made her move.

Using the braid as a handle, Ramone pulled Dog around and slapped her down hard on her stomach. The young woman hit the floor hard. Once again, all of the torture devices worked hideously against her. One nipple clamp was knocked loose against the floor, and Dog screamed into the gag; she thought her nipple had been torn away with it. The injured breast burned as much without the clamp as with it. The other one continued to bite hard into her flesh. It was clasped firmly on the nipple, trapped on her breast, with her own weight holding it down.

"Would you like to?" Slash held the belt out.

"With pleasure." Ramone shook the belt again; she knew how experienced submissives could often judge their torture devices by the sounds they made. She knew she was right when she saw Dog's face flush and her hands clasp and open. Dog's back was pale and smooth, and the black strap and metal rod stood out boldly against her skin. Ramone selected her position carefully and lifted her arm.

The belt was devious because, once it struck, it wrapped itself around its victim. This was an interesting situation because of the metal rod, and both Ramone and Slash were intrigued by it.

Ramone brought the belt down hard. It caught Dog's side and smacked painfully against her ribs. As it snaked across her body, it hit the rod with a resounding crack. Dog was spared the bite of leather right on her spine.

But the belt struck again on the other side of the rod. It came down on Dog's ribs on the far side. The pointed end of the supple leather belt wrapped around so completely from the force of Ramone's strike that the tip actually left a bright red crescent on the side of Dog's breast, which was flattened under her against the floor.

The young woman's body convulsed, as if from electric shock. She groaned loudly into the ball gag and trembled all over, while Ramone and Slash admired the result.

Dog's skin was pale and the marks showed up like painted lines. There was one red welt the width of the belt that went from Dog's side and up over her back, just below her shoulder blades. It stopped abruptly a few inches from the metal rod. A second one started the same distance away on the other side. It curved lusciously around her flank and ended with the bright red half-moon on the white skin of Dog's battered breast.

Ramone lifted her arm again. This time the belt came down across Dog's shoulders. The young woman moaned again. Her hands convulsed helplessly in their chains. She tried to move her legs, but could not. Ramone waited several minutes before delivering a third blow just above her kidneys. Blindfolded, Dog had no idea when the next blow was coming. The minutes seemed like hours to her; the horrid stripe was almost a relief from the incessant waiting and the tension it created.

A total of six stripes were given her with the belt. Ramone admired them and looked forward to removing the rod that went up the young woman's spine and held her arms in their cramped position. The pale back would be covered with welts that all stopped at precisely the same spot on either side of her backbone—a most intriguing sight for a Mistress to see.

"Would you like a turn?" Ramone asked. Dog shivered. This unknown, unseen Mistress had been nasty, and Dog knew that Slash would naturally try to top her. That was the worst part about serving more than one Mistress at the same time; it became a competition between the dominatrixes. Dog always remembered, with a hot twinge of sexual satisfaction deep in her pussy, the night that she had laid naked on the floor with four of them over her. Dog hadn't been able to walk properly for a week after that.

Slash took the belt. It was warm; she could almost feel the satisfaction of Ramone's solid blows in its length. She shook it again to make the buckle jangle, and then she held it in the middle.

Her target was Dog's tight, nicely rounded buttocks, and her blow fell right across them. Dog screamed into the ball gag and gasped, trying not to black out. Slash had hit her with the buckle.

This was no ordinary punishment. The buckle tore into the flesh and the tongue drew a bright line that stayed in place for just a second and then seeped a small gash of thin blood.

"I like it," Slash said. Ramone noticed that the black woman was running her hand over her own flat belly, her fingers moving closer and closer to that spot between her legs.

"You always knew how to bring out the best in a submissive," Ramone agreed, and then watched as Slash brought out a trickle of blood on the other perfect, pale buttock with the nasty chrome tongue of the buckle.

"I think I'm ready for some nice raw sushi now," Slash said.

She reached down and pulled on the braid, which now seemed to be placed there conveniently for their use alone. Dog only whimpered when she was dragged back up into a sitting position on the floor. Her wrists hung almost lifelessly in the shackles, and her pussy was numb with the huge dildo distending it. She hardly even noticed when Ramone picked up the nipple clamp that had fallen off and reattached it to the swollen nub at the end of Dog's breast. They left her like that, still blindfolded, but still in a state of unimaginable excitement that she was the focus of attention for these two magnificent Mistresses.

Arm in arm, the two women walked across the loft to Slash's bedroom. Their heels rang on the hardwood floor and Dog's spirits fell as she realized that they were walking away from her. She wanted to please them so! She consoled herself by reveling in the fiery pain that radiated from her striped back and her injured asscheeks.

When they got to the bed, Slash turned to Ramone and started to undress her. Ramone stood there and let her, not lifting a finger to assist. It was a delicious feeling to be completely under the control of this amazing woman.

Completely naked, Ramone was stretched out on the bed. Slash turned to the small table where all of her equipment had been put out beforehand.

A small snowy-white towel was put under Ramone's luscious buttocks to protect the bed. Slash ran her fingers over Ramone's enticingly hairy pussy, tweaking the spiky hairs gently and stroking the ever-enlarging clit with the very end of her fingernail. Ramone sighed as the touch thrilled her entire body.

"You've still got too much on," Slash said. "I like to see you completely naked."

Ramone smiled at her. "Wasn't that why you asked me here?"

Slash kissed her fingertips and then pressed them to Ramone's pussy. "You know I always ask first."

From the table she took a mug and an expensive natural-bristled, wooden-handled shaving brush. There was a ceramic bowl of warm water, and she dipped the bristles into it. The mug had a disc of shaving soap in it. She stirred it up to obtain a thick, creamy lather.

She used the brush to cover Ramone's pussy. The Japanese woman sighed at the warmth of the lather between her legs. It was the perfect trade-off: Slash loved to wield the razor, and Ramone loved the feeling of just lying back and letting it all happen.

Slash took much longer than was actually necessary to soap up Ramone's cunt, but there were no objections. Slash was a sculptor, and the cream was her medium; she used the brush to tease it into curves and curls, to build up thick ridges of cream at the opening to Ramone's slit and cover everything until just the very ends of the hairs stuck through the white covering. Slash loved to shave, loved everything about it. More than once she had taken half the night just to get Ramone's pussy hairless.

Her instrument was in an ebony box, and she opened the lid almost reverently. Disposable plastic safety razors were for amateurs. From the box Slash took a gleaming, ivory-handled straight razor.

She opened it and the blade glinted in the light. There was no need to hone it, for the edge on it was perfect. Having been shaved clean by the blade many times before, Ramone was completely relaxed. She had total faith in her companion's ability.

Slash started at the top of Ramone's hairline, on the flat part of her mound just below her belly. She used tiny movements of the razor, taking out just a few hairs at a time, and going over the same spot several times until the skin was completely bare. Each tiny area had to be absolutely clean before she moved on to the next.

As careful as she was there, she was even more meticulous on the folds of Ramone's cunt. The razor was dipped continually into the bowl of hot water, and Ramone languished in the ecstasy of the warm steel and Slash's fingers teasing her pussy. The lather near her hole was diluted with the hot juice that oozed out as she became more and more excited.

Slash's own cunt was throbbing. She breathed deeply. She squeezed her thighs together to give herself a rush, but other than that, she had to ignore it. No matter how much she wanted to put her hand between her legs and rub hard on her soaked slit, she kept her mind on what she was doing. This was just too delicate a process to risk nicking the pussy entrusted into her care.

The hair and foam built up in the ceramic bowl as Ramone's completely naked skin emerged. Some of the shaving cream had strayed onto the inside of Ramone's thighs. Slash removed it from the skin expertly with long, languishing strokes of the straight razor. Ramone shivered with delight at the long lap of steel against her leg.

With meticulous precision and strokes so tiny that the razor hardly moved, Slash cleaned away the foam and some stray hairs from around Ramone's tightly puckered asshole. A few final flicks of the blade, and Ramone's pussy was completely devoid of hair and lather.

"How does it look?" Ramone asked as Slash rinsed off the razor, drying it carefully. Now completely naked, she reached down to touch herself. She loved the feeling when Slash shaved her. Not only was it nice on her fingertips, but her pussy throbbed at the touch of bare skin on equally bare skin.

"As good as it always does," Slash replied throatily.

The sight of a shaved pussy was one of Slash's ultimate turn-ons. It looked innocent and virginal and at the same time, deliciously slutty and raw. Now the lips really did look like lips, jutting out and down from Ramone's mound, the slit of the mouth between them ready to take Slash's tongue into its throat. In a way, it seemed almost strange, for without the hair inching up from her crotch, it made Ramone's cunt seem twice as long, twice as far away from her navel. It looked foreign, unusual, not the way a grown woman was supposed to look. Perhaps it was the strangeness that turned Slash on, but for now, she was not about to dwell on analyzing her sexual perspectives. All she wanted to do was eat.

There was one final ritual, one that both Slash and Ramone looked forward to. They had been doing it for so long that neither could remember why Slash did it, but for both of them it had become a necessary finale.

Slash held up her hand. A single silver ring glinted on one long dark finger. With the other she picked up the gleaming razor and held it over the cunt she had just shaved clean.

She brought her hands together with the razor against her index finger. Both held their breath as the cruel edge of the blade nicked the flesh of Slash's finger.

Slash put the razor down and pressed hard on her finger. A single drop of blood appeared on the edge. She pressed until it was too heavy and dropped onto Ramone's skin, right at the very top of Ramone's freshly shaven slit.

The bright crimson drop formed a perfect sphere on the smooth olive skin. Slash admired it for a long time. It started to elongate and slide toward the division of Ramone's naked slit. Just before it did, Slash caught it with the very tip of her tongue.

It was hot in her mouth, but nowhere near the searing temperature of Ramone's slit. Slash lapped up and down the length of her cunt. The unusual smoothness, along with the slight soapy tang left from the shaving cream, excited her so much that she had to press her own clit with her fingers through the electric-blue suit.

Ramone squirmed in ecstasy herself on the huge bed. Normally, the hair acted like a buffer, protecting her skin from Slash's touch. Now each movement of her lover's tongue was brand-new. It seemed as if she had always been eaten through her clothes and now, for the first time, the touch was directly on her body. She felt totally, completely naked, and she knew it wouldn't take long to come.

Slash knew it, too, and was determined to make it last. She spent the longest time just going up and down the smooth lips, staying on either side of the sex-swollen flesh in between. She went nowhere near the clit that had grown so large that it was pushing its way out of the folds to demand attention.

She toyed with the rosebud of Ramone's ass, licking at this forbidden delight, and pressed her tongue in hard until she could feel it pass through the tight ring of muscle into the superheated, velvety chamber. Ramone groaned and Slash had to finger herself even harder through her suit to ease the throbbing. Her belly was full of want, and she knew that she had to make herself come. She simply couldn't wait much longer.

Gradually she moved up to the next hole and fucked Ramone's vagina with her tongue as well. Ramone groaned at the full, wet, rimmed feeling and tried to get Slash to move up to her clit, but to no avail. Slash was in control here, and Ramone was just going to have to lie back and enjoy it. Realizing this, she did.

Slash stayed a long time here, until her mouth seemed filled to overflow with the pussyjuice that Ramone's needy cunt was producing. The fluid was sweet as wine and Slash couldn't get enough of it. She wanted to lie in it, to bathe in it. She wanted to drown in it.

Fina!ly, just as Ramone neared the point of being unable to take any more, Slash took her tongue out of the hairless hole and moved it ever so slowly up to the top. She stopped at the huge, hard nub of Ramone's needy clit.

The flesh was swollen to three times its usual size with sexual want. Ramone almost jumped out of her skin when Slash touched it. No matter how many times Slash took the straight razor and shaved her skin, it was always like the first when her smooth pussy was eaten afterward.

"That's so good!" she moaned as she writhed on the bed. She almost felt high. Her fingers found her own tits automatically, and she twisted the nipples firmly. The luscious feeling of movement on both her cunt and her tits echoed throughout her whole body.

Slash groaned herself. Her fingers were now moving just as hard and fast on her own clit. She had kept on the form-fitting blue suit, and she rubbed herself through the fabric. It was an unusual feeling, exactly the opposite of Ramone's completely naked pussy, and Slash reveled in the excitement of a change. The fabric molded itself to her fingers and to her clit, and glided smoothly over both.

She came just a split second after Ramone did. Ramone was close to coming, so close that she was almost insane. She lifted her ass off the bed, bucked her hips to slide her cunt up and down in Slash's mouth, grabbed her lover's head, and tried to pull her deep inside. She screamed and cried out as the need built up to an almost-unbearable throbbing inside of her. Slash put her lips right on Ramone's clit and sucked hard, sucked it in between her teeth, sucked the fluid off it even as her tongue pushed it back and forth. Ramone screamed her pleasure as it all exploded deep in her cunt.

Slash stayed with her even as her own body rocked with the tremors of her own orgasm. She continued to rub the soaked fabric into her cunt, continued to eat Ramone's pussy. Only when the last convulsions went through both of them did they stop.

Slash fell on to the bed, to lie beside the gasping and moaning Ramone. Both of them felt completely drained, completely satisfied. They tried to catch their breath, and their chests rose and fell with the effort. When they had calmed down enough, they shared a long kiss and held each other tightly.

"You're amazing!" Ramone smiled and ran her hands over Slash's body. The blue suit was silky, and her hand glided over it smoothly. It was such a luscious feeling that she continued until she had rubbed her all over, stopping to pay particular attention to the nipples that stuck out hard through the fabric. Between her legs, the suit was soaked with pussyjuice. Ramone rubbed hard until it was on her own fingers. Then she slowly licked them clean.

Slash reached down to cup Ramone's pussy with her hand. Without the hair, the skin felt twice as warm as usual. She didn't stroke or caress, but simply kept her hand there, enjoying the unique feeling of perfectly smooth skin that would normally be spiky with thick black hair.

As much as she loved the act of shaving, however, it was something she did only with her equals. No submissive would ever submit to her straight razor, even if she were tied down with her arms and legs shackled to the four posts of the bed. This would never be a punishment, only a reward. For Slash, it was too intimate an act ever to be wasted on such scum as a slave.

They stayed together on the bed for a long time. "I suppose your little friend is in pretty rough shape by now," Ramone said.

Slash laughed. "I'd totally forgotten about it," she said. "You're probably right. Oh, well, its personal well-being is no concern of mine."

The tall woman got up and went into the kitchen, where she started up the coffeemaker. Other than the refrigerator, which seldom held more than a few bottles of water or leftover takeout, it was the only appliance that ever got used in the professional kitchen. Slash firmly believed that there were enough people in the city more than willing to make dinner in their restaurants for her.

When the coffee was ready, she filled two mugs and set them on the heavy pine table. The light from the huge windows poured in and showed off the gleaming wooden top. Slash never hired for cleaners, but her loft was always spotless. When it needed attention, she simply picked up a submissive who looked in need of commanding, and ordered her to scrub and polish.

Dog was still in her sitting position on the floor, although it was obvious that very little was keeping her upright. The shackles on her ankles kept her legs together, so she was unable to shift her position and fall over. Her arms slumped lifelessly in their chains and her head was down, as if she didn't have the strength to hold it upright. But she lifted it quickly enough when she realized that the two Mistresses were back in the room with her and scrutinizing her carefully.

"Absolutely marvelous," Ramone said. The wide stripes on her back, made by the leather belt, had turned a hideous mottled purple. What they could see of her buttocks was also horribly bruised. Even the crescent on her tit, caused by the tip of the leather belt coming around and smacking hard, was as bright as it had ever been. The two were sure that Dog would carry it that way for at least a week.

Slash had further plans for this one; once her streak of cruelty was tapped, it knew few bounds.

She opened the shackles that kept Dog's ankles together, although the leather straps and the short chain remained there. Then she unbuckled the blindfold.

Dog opened her eyes, and then shut them again quickly, against the light that flooded the room. "Open them!" Slash commanded. Dog squinted, then forced them open as Slash's shoe connected with her bruised buttocks. Her eyes flooded with tears as the light burned them and she blinked several times, but managed to obey.

"I recognize it now," Ramone said, as she got her first look at the young woman's face, mottled from the blindfold, still distended by the ball gag. "It's been hanging around for a few days, hasn't it?"

"That's right," Slash said. "I think it's new around here. Doesn't matter where it came from, though; I just thought I'd have a bit of fun with it."

She reached down and grabbed the convenient braid. She was very strong, and Dog didn't have a chance to scramble up as it was pulled. It wouldn't have done her much good, anyway, as her cramped legs refused to respond. Slash pulled her up to her feet and then let go of her hair. The young woman, unable to put out her shackled hands to break her fall, crumpled and fell hard to the ground.

Ramone shook her head. "They don't make them very hardy anymore, do they?" she said.

"Not at all," Slash said. "Oh, well, I guess I'll just have to drag it."

That was exactly what she did, as Dog tried hard to get to her feet. She could not, and Slash dragged her across the floor by her hair until they reached the huge window opposite the pine table.

The window had a very wide ledge, with a chrome ring screwed into the wood. As Dog's eyes opened in fear, the tall black woman picked her up by the hair and one numb arm, and lifted her onto the ledge. Standing on the ledge herself, Slash pulled the young woman to her feet and stood there for a minute, supporting her, until the feeling came back into Dog's legs and she was able to stand by herself.

Once that was accomplished, Slash got down off the ledge and snapped the chain attached to Dog's ankle strap to the chrome ring. As a final indignity, she pulled the huge dildo out of Dog's pussy. The young woman sighed with relief as the rubber penis was removed, but groaned again as Slash pulled her battered asscheeks apart roughly and shoved the dildo deep into her anus. Slash was quick to notice, with a nod to Ramone, that the dildo was well lubricated with pussyjuice. For all her misery, the young submissive was excited. Slash then ordered her to look out of the window.

Dog shrieked through the ball gag as she looked down. The loft was over Rough Trade, and the window faced a busy New York street. The sidewalks were filled with pedestrians. The road was jammed with cars.

Anyone looking up at the second-floor window would instantly see a young woman standing there, completely naked, her arms outstretched and held up by chains attached to a pole up her spine. They would see a dog collar around her neck and nipple clamps biting into the tender nubs of her breasts. They would see her mouth held open by a ball gag. They would not be able to see the stripes from the leather belt or the thin lines of dried blood on her asscheeks, but they would witness her suffering.

Slash counted on three things. First, no one in New York ever looked up when they were walking, and secondly, if they did see Dog, they wouldn't do anything about it. Of course, both of these points were negated by the third, which was that Slash didn't really give a shit who saw her.

Dog knew none of this. All she knew was that she was on public display, in regalia that she wore proudly but only in private. She sobbed into the ball gag. Then, in a futile and childish gesture, she screwed her eyes shut. Perhaps, if she couldn't see them, they couldn't see her.

Slash noticed immediately. "Do you know how eye surgery is done?" she asked the young woman pleasantly.

Dog shook her head.

Slash explained patiently, as if to a young child. "When eye surgery is done, the eye has to be completely open," she said. "The doctor uses special clamps that keep the eyelids from closing. Now, I happen to have a pair of them. We don't want to be using them, do we?"

Dog's eyes did open wide, this time in horror. As Slash walked back to the table, she gave Ramone a mischievous wink, and they both smiled as co-conspirators. These submissives were so stupid! They could be led to believe anything. Of course, Ramone was going by the wink. If she hadn't seen it, it wouldn't have surprised her to know that Slash did indeed have such ghastly instruments in her possession.

They drank their coffee slowly, enjoying the suffering of the young woman who watched every pedestrian with a cold terror in her gut. If one even looked around, she broke into a sweat.

"I wanted to pick up a few things before I open the bar," Slash said as she finished her coffee. "Care to come with me?"

"Sure," Ramone said. They went into the bedroom and dressed for the street. When they came back out, Slash got up on the ledge and unbuckled Dog's ball gag slowly, letting it fall to the floor where it bounced and rolled away.

It was some time before the young woman could close her mouth, and even then it was with great difficulty and a harsh cracking of her jawbone. She worked her jaw from side to side, trying to get some normal feeling back into it.

"I don't know when we'll be back," Slash said. "If I were you, I wouldn't think about moving." It didn't take long for Dog to realize her meaning. The chrome ring she was snapped to was set high above the floor. If she moved, she would fall backward, hung up by her leg to the ring. With her arms chained at the height of her shoulders, she would not be able to unsnap the tether. She would only be able to stand there helplessly, unable to move. Further, she knew that if Slash found that she had disobeyed, she was sure she would remain there hanging all day and all night.

"Please, Mistress!" she sobbed. "Please, mercy, Mistress! Please don't make me stay in the window, please…!"

Under any other circumstances, both Slash and Ramone would have punished her heartily and instantly for speaking without permission. In this case, they let it go. It was just too much fun to hear her pleading, hear the desperation in her voice. When they stopped and cruelly waved good-bye to her from the street, looking up at the chained, naked, tortured woman in the window, her mouth still begged the words they could not hear. Slash just smiled. It would be one more thing to punish her for when they returned.

Chapter Six

A Harley-Davidson pulling up at the front of Rough Trade was not an unusual occurrence, but the woman who got off it was certainly the center of attention for the women standing outside the door.

Her name was Sondra and she pulled the huge machine back onto its stand as effortlessly as if it had been a bicycle. It was even more amazing because she was petite and seemed far too small to even be able to handle the bike at all.

Handle it she did, and admirably. She hung her helmet on the bike and shook out her long, wavy hair. There were women on the sidewalk waiting to get into the bar and Sondra knew they were watching her, so she made the most of it. She put her hands under the bulk of her mane and shook it out, spreading it across her back. Her piercing gray eyes sized up the spectators as she did, and they admired her thin, delicate features that were at such odds with her enormous strength and cool expression.

Some of the leatherwomen were cupping their own breasts needily at the sight of Sondra's costume. Her leathers were well worn, the black faded almost gray from constant riding. Her jacket was adorned with heavy chrome chains and when she unzipped it, she had a leather vest on under it. The vest was open; there was nothing beneath that. Her tits were small but very firm and the nipples were rockhard from rubbing against the leather.

Her jeans were equally worn, the ass almost white, and they fit her like a second skin. She wore leather chaps over them. When she turned around, the women could see the way the black leather straps buckled high under her asscheeks. With the jacket ending at her waist, the buttocks wrapped tightly in denim, and the leather strapped under, it was an ass worthy of admiration.

The effect was rounded out with a pair of motorcycle boots. They were heavy black leather as well, and had obviously seen as many miles as Sondra's other clothes, but these had had considerable attention lavished on them. They were polished to a high gloss, even in the tiny cracks over her toes, and the heels were new. Leather straps and chains went around the ankles and under the heel, and they clanked on the sidewalk as she moved. They were heavy boots, nasty boots, and more than one woman waiting on the sidewalk wondered if Sondra had lovingly polished them herself, or another woman had been forced to. Many of them wished desperately that she could be commanded to do such a job.

The women who were on the sidewalk were waiting to be allowed into the bar; it was too crowded inside, and they had to wait for enough people to come out before the bouncer at the door would allow them in. Sondra walked up the line; she knew every eye was on her, waiting to see what she was going to do.

One of the women standing there was obviously submissive, and when Sondra looked at her, the young woman dropped her eyes instinctively and stared at the sidewalk. Sondra liked the look of this one, and she came closer.

"Out for a night on the town, chickie?" she asked.

The woman nodded, but still did not look up. She was wearing tight jeans and a silk shirt, and she stiffened but said nothing when Sondra grabbed her tits through the shirt with both hands. The leather-clad woman squeezed the nipples so hard that the submissive woman gasped. Then she reached down to cup the woman's pussy with her fingers. "Not bad," she said. And, just as abruptly, she let go and kept walking down the line. The woman looked after her, with a strange expression, half-relieved that she was no longer the center of this strange woman's attention, and at the same time, disappointed because she was not.

The woman at the door was a tough butch, chosen specifically for her attitude. Sondra ignored her completely and walked past her into the bar.

"Hey!" the butch yelled. "Hey, where do you think you're going?"

Sondra looked at her, her face expressionless. "I'm thirsty," she said. "This is a bar. I'm going in for a beer."

"Everybody in this lineup is thirsty," the butch said. "You've got to wait your turn, honey. Everybody does."

Sondra kept walking. "I'm not everybody," she said.

The butch spun around and grabbed Sondra's leather jacket. Sondra turned quickly but kept her cool. She spoke low through her teeth, menacingly icy, completely in control. "Don't lay your hands on me. Nobody touches me unless I touch them first. You understand?"

"I touch anyone I want," the butch insisted. "Now get to the back of the line."

"Fuck you!" Sondra said. "I'm paying for my beer. I'm going in to get it."

Their voices were raised and Slash, behind the bar, noticed them. Leaving the pouring duties to Ramone, she came out from behind and walked over to the door. Her height and her obvious strength were intensified by the red leather catsuit and the heavy boots she wore.

Sondra and the butch bouncer were very close to blows. Slash stood over both of them and said loudly, "Is there a problem here?"

Both turned to look at her, and the butch loosened her grip on Sondra's jacket slightly. Sondra pulled it away and straightened it. "Not much of one," she said. "Your bulldyke here doesn't think I should have a beer."

Slash sized everything up immediately: the bouncer, the biker in her leather suit, the lineup outside. She was just about to throw the brassy woman out until she looked down at her.

The leather chaps framed the crotch of Sondra's tight jeans. Slash noticed the bulge beneath the fly immediately. The woman's crotch was packed, and Slash liked that. This pushy woman might turn out to be entertaining.

Slash looked over Sondra's head. "It's okay," she said to the bouncer. "I invited her. I'm sorry, I forgot to tell you." Face saved, the bouncer turned away, back to the lineup outside the door.

Slash led the woman to the bar. "You're new here, aren't you?" she asked.

"Just in from L.A.," Sondra said. "I thought I'd see if all the rumors about this place were true."

Slash looked at her, then around the bar. Women were groping on the dance floor; many of them were dancing half-naked, and some had no clothes on at all. Several women in the booths were obviously having sex together. A Mistress was leading a submissive into the back, to one of the rooms with the table and the rings set into the wall. "I think you'll find that no one ever has to exaggerate about Rough Trade," she said.

Sondra went to the front of the bar, where two women moved aside to make room for her. Slash went behind. "A beer," Sondra said, and Slash didn't even bother to ask what brand. She knew it wouldn't be necessary. She put up a popular one; without pausing, Sondra drained half the bottle.

"So what's the scene like out in California these days?" Slash asked. She found herself drawn to this biker woman, whose attitude so closely resembled her own.

"Well, we don't have anything like this," Sondra said. She finished the bottle of beer and looked over with a meaningful expression. Slash uncapped another and put it on the bar; Sondra drank this one slowly. "This place is all they talk about out there. Every dyke in the city knows about it. I was thinking about coming to New York to look up an old friend, and this was one more reason to hop on the bike and ride out."

Slash looked at her. "Good choice."

She pointed down to Sondra's crotch. "I notice you're packing something in those jeans. Going to let me in on the secret?"

Sondra smiled at her. "I thought you'd never ask."

Their attention was caught by a commotion on the

dance floor. The couples on there had made a circle around one pair, and all were watching them. Both were naked to the waist, their jeans tight around their asses. They were arguing over a third woman, young, blonde, who stood back, her eyes wide, frightened.

No one moved to break them up, and their voices rose in fury. The third young woman looked back and forth at both of them, completely unsure of what to do. By the fact that both were dressed the same, their naked tits jiggling as they argued, Slash gathered that they had come in together, but one had found the sweet blonde stranger more appealing than her date.

The taller of the two threw the first punch. She connected with her partner's stomach, and the woman doubled over. This gave an opportunity for a shot to the jaw that sent her reeling.

The injured woman was scrappy, though, and she was up in a second. She ran straight at her opponent and butted her, knocking her down. As she fell, the other was on her instantly.

Ramone started to leave the bar to break up the fight, but Slash stopped her. "Let it go awhile. The floor show doesn't start for another hour." Ramone relaxed, and stood back to do what she had wanted all along, which was to watch the two dykes battle over the blonde pussy one had picked up in the bar.

The one on top reached down and seized the bare tits below her. She squeezed as hard as she could. Her fingers sank into the flesh. The downed woman screamed in pain and anger and tried to buck her off. Her hands flailed and connected, but the woman on top was tough, and she warded off the blows with one hand. With the other, she kept punishing the breast she was squeezing.

Slash could actually see the flesh turn purple with

bruises under her fingers. With a huge effort, the woman lifted her body and, at the same time, brought her fist up. The fighter on top lost her balance and they rolled on the floor, each trying to gain the upper hand.

The taller one got it. She punched her assailant several times, until the woman had had enough and dropped her hands. There was a final spiteful blow, and then the taller woman pushed her opponent away in disgust.

She stood up, breathing hard, and wiped a trickle of blood off her lip with the back of her hand. Five dark bruises marred her breast where it had been grabbed. The other woman, bruised, bleeding, dazed, got up slowly. Passing the table where they had been sitting, she picked up her shirt from the back of her chair and slunk out of the bar.

The victor turned to her spoils, the young woman who had been the cause of the fight. Her eyes gleamed as she realized that the woman who had originally come on to her had also won the right to have her, and she stepped out of the crowd toward her.

It was too much for Sondra, who had spent the short time the fight had gone on with her hand over the bulge in her crotch, rubbing it slowly. "I want that," she said. "I really want that. I think I'm going to have a piece of that."

She winked at Slash as she put down her beer bottle and moved away from the bar. The circle was still open in the crowd on the dance floor, and Sondra walked into it. Without a word, seemingly oblivious to the fact that the tall, bruised woman was standing there watching, she walked up to the young woman who had been the cause of the fight and felt her breast right through her shirt.

There were gasps from the crowd, from women who were amazed at her nerve, and from women anticipating another battle. To say that both the fighter and her prize were shocked was an understatement. To Sondra it was simply something she had to do.

"Hey!" The shock worn off, the bruised fighter took a menacing step toward Sondra.

Sondra turned and simply looked at her with her cold gray eyes. Despite her slight build, her biker attitude, along with the road-weary leather clothes, made her seem larger and tougher. She took one step forward, and the chains on her boots clanked on the polished floor.

Her opponent stopped, seemingly confused. Sondra pointedly fingered the chain that snaked through the strap on her shoulder and down across the front of her jacket. The woman could see that the strap was held closed with only a small snap, and that in an instant, Sondra could whip the heavy chrome chain off her jacket and wield it as a deadly weapon.

It was too much, and the fighter knew she was beaten even before any trouble started. She stood still for just a moment, just enough to uphold her place in the pecking order among the regulars in the bar. Her breasts still moved gloriously with her heavy breathing. One breast was stained with purple bruises, and her face was swollen and bruised. She made sure everyone knew she had beaten her first opponent. Then she turned and, like the first woman, picked up her shirt and walked away.

All eyes were now on Sondra and the young woman. Sondra assessed her prize. She was so blonde that her short hair was almost white. Frightened again, her eyes opened wide with disbelief as Sondra undid the buttons of her shirt casually and threw it open in front of the crowd. She then fondled the naked breasts and tweaked the nipples.

Taking off her jacket and tossing it on the floor, she pulled back her open vest and rubbed her own rockhard nipples against the pale ones she had taken for her own.

As she drew in close, she straddled the blonde woman's leg and pushed her packed crotch against it. She rubbed up and down on the pale thigh, pressing her breasts against the shirtless ones at the same time. She was humping the blonde's leg, but now everyone could see that there was more in those jeans than just a pussy. The dance floor was packed with women standing shoulder to shoulder, the ones behind craning their necks impatiently to see. They all were curious, and all were turned on. The whole room smelled of sex, of hot, wet pussies in need of coming.

Abruptly Sondra pushed the blonde woman away and down, so that she fell on her knees to the floor. Her face was at the level of Sondra's heavy belt buckle, at the level of those chaps and at the fly of those packed jeans.

Everyone was watching and waiting. Sondra unzipped the jeans dramatically and reached into them. She fished inside, tugged, and finally released a huge black rubber cock.

Her impromptu audience murmured its approval. The dildo was enormous. Sondra stroked it lovingly. She turned around completely and pointed it at the women surrounding her. She cupped the huge knob on the end and pulled her fly farther apart to show off the heavy balls that were attached.

Then she turned again, and stuck it in the blonde woman's face. "Suck me," she said. "Suck me off. Make me come."

The crowd cheered. The blonde woman looked at it, unsure; it really was huge. Her uncertainty was something that Sondra would not tolerate. She reached down and grabbed the back of her head. She stuck the cock right on the blonde's closed lips and pushed her hips forward to force it in.

The blonde woman choked a little at first, but then got used to its size in her mouth. It quickly went from being punishment to pleasure.

She fellated the cock hungrily and Sondra encouraged her. She fucked the blonde's mouth slowly. The cock slid in between those sweet lips, distended with its size, and the black rubber looked almost nasty against her pale skin. The woman's tongue slipped out between her lips to wrap around the thick shaft. Sondra pulled it out just as slowly, wet with saliva, until the knob was right at her lips, about to slip out completely. Then she moved her hips and put the cock right back in again.

Sondra's hand was around the base of the rubber dildo, her fingers running over the soft, meaty balls. Her other hand was around her breasts, and she fingered her own nipples. She could see several of the women in the crowd doing the same thing, either to themselves or to women beside them. One couple seemed down each other's throats with their tongues, their hands in each other's cunts. Sondra loved it, and she fucked her cocksucker faster.

Before long, her hips were a blur. The cock was pounding in and out of her mouth. The blonde's lips were now open wide and she let the cock fuck her while her tongue flashed over it. She had her own hand between her legs, playing with her clit through the fabric of her tight jeans. She could smell Sondra's leather, taste the rubber, feel her fingers. Everything seemed to be played out for her benefit alone.

Sondra was breathing hard now, groaning as if she were about to come. "So good!" she cried out, and then she pulled back, out of the blonde's mouth, and squeezed the rubber balls as hard as she could.

A hot stream of thick white fluid spurted out of the hole at the end of the cock, all over the blonde's face. The woman snapped back for a moment, surprised. Then she leaned forward and let the hot come splash all over her cheeks and mouth.

The crowd roared its approval. The rubber cock spurted and pulsed, over and over, releasing an almost-impossible amount of white come. It covered the blonde's face and dripped down to her naked breasts, covering them. Finally, the come all spent, Sondra groaned again and shook the cock to release the last few precious drops.

She put the knob of the cock back at the blonde's mouth, expectantly. The woman responded immediately by taking it into her mouth and licking it clean. Once it was, she licked her lips; she didn't know what the liquid was, but it was warm and salty-sweet, and she savored it.

Sondra was done with her now and turned away. As soon as she did, another woman broke from the crowd and knelt beside the blonde, kissing her deeply to get the taste of the come from her tongue. The blonde pulled away and looked up beseechingly at Sondra, eager for more from this intriguing, exciting woman, but Sondra ignored her. The blonde looked hurt for just a moment, and then turned back to her new companion and continued to kiss, kneeling on the hard floor of the bar, watched from every angle by the crowd. That was the best thing about Rough Trade: if you couldn't get what you wanted from one woman, there were always more waiting to take her place.

Slash and Ramone looked at each other, both of them incredibly hot. "That's one act I haven't seen in here yet," Ramone said.

"Not bad at all," Slash agreed, reaching to touch her lover's tit through the T-shirt she wore. "Maybe that's one we should consider for our nightly entertainment."

Neither of them noticed Kiki, in her disc-jockey booth, until the music stopped. Kiki had been aware of the fight and of the subsequent excitement on the barroom floor, but because of the crowd of people packed around it she had not been able to see any of the action. Now the leather-clad biker walked through the crowd and Kiki just stared in disbelief. Then she came out of her surprise-induced daze. She grabbed the microphone and cried out, "Sondra!" It reverberated throughout the entire bar.

Sondra spun around, wondering where the sound had come from. She spied the disc-jockey booth and the rail-thin, blue-haired woman who was bouncing up and down in it. "Kiki!"

They met halfway as Kiki tore open the booth door and ran out, in a hug so strong that they twirled around several times before Kiki's feet hit the floor again. They kissed several times, hurriedly, as if they had to get in as many as possible in the time they had. Only then, when hugs and kisses were exchanged, did they stand back and simply look at each other.

"Skinnier than ever!" Sondra said. "And I think your hair was pink the last time I saw you. Girl, why didn't you tell me you were working here?"

"It hasn't been that long." Kiki smiled, the ball pierced through her tongue glinting in the colored lights. "Besides, I didn't know you were coming out here, or I would have told you. How was I supposed to know you were going to show up in New York?"

"Well, you know me," Sondra said. "I just got up one morning and decided the bike needed a good run.

When I got far enough north, I made up my mind to come to New York. I figured I'd look you up once I got here. So I guess I don't have to go to that trouble now."

Kiki reached down and grabbed the thick cock, which was still sticking out of Sondra's fly. "It's been too long since I've seen that," she said. "I wasn't sure if you were still into that scene."

Sondra smiled. "Want to see if I still am?"

Kiki didn't have to say a word; she simply led Sondra into the disc-jockey booth, much to the disappointment of several women standing near it who would have given anything for a chance to go inside with the petite leather-clad biker.

They still got quite a show, since the two never even bothered to close the booth door behind them. Kiki was wearing tight shorts and a cropped shirt, which she slipped out of in seconds. Sondra also stripped, leaving on just the leather vest. The thick black dildo was held in place with leather straps that clung to her hips. Kiki quickly threw in a CD with some pounding music on it, a long one that she wouldn't have to change for a while.

Along with the equipment and the boxes of records and CDs, Kiki also had a small table with some papers on it. Sondra pushed these aside with a quick sweep of her arm. She held Kiki tightly and they kissed, their lips mashed against each other and their tongues meeting and thrusting. She backed her lover against the table and laid her down on it, spreading her thighs apart with her knees as she did.

The cock slid smoothly into Kiki's wet cunt. She groaned as the thickness of it spread her wide open and the knob pushed in deep. Sondra put her hands on Kiki's small tits and kneaded them, and Kiki reached up to do the same.

Sondra was an expert at the meaning of "well and truly fucked." She handled the cock as if it were her own. She swooped in from above to rub it against Kiki's clit and then fucked her so fast and hard that her hips were a blur. Kiki reached behind to grab Sondra's tight, sweet asscheeks and pull them even closer to herself. Each time the cock slid in all the way, until the latex balls slapped firmly against Sondra's ass. They were so soaked with pussyjuice that the slaps sounded wet.

"It's all out of jism!" Sondra moaned. "I used it all on that blonde bitch out there. If I'd known you were here I would have saved you some!"

Kiki was panting so hard, it was difficult to make out her words. "Then I'll just have to make you come a different way!"

The rhythm of the music was all-encompassing and Sondra fucked along with the fast beat. In and out, in and out, she pounded into Kiki's cunt, slammed against her clit, slapped the balls against her ass. She could almost feel the friction of the cockskin against Kiki's tunnel walls. She wished she could stick the cock right into her own mound, make it part of her own body and fuck Kiki completely.

Her tits, half-covered with black leather, rubbed all over Kiki's chest as they jiggled with her movements. Her asscheeks tightened with each thrust. The straps strained against her hips with the pressure.

Kiki's moan grew louder. By the flush on her chest and the hardness of her nipples, Sondra could tell that she was close to coming. "Fuck me harder! Harder! Fuck me, please!" she cried out, and Sondra was only too happy to oblige. She groaned with the exertion. She could feel each slap of the balls against Kiki's ass throughout her whole body.

"You're going to...I'm going to come!" Kiki screamed. She howled out her pleasure over the pounding rhythms of the music and the black dildo. She writhed on the table and grabbed her own nipples and squeezed them. It was followed a second later by another wave, another orgasm that swept right through her.

She was too excited to lie back and relax. She knew Sondra so well that they moved as one. Sondra moved back one step, pulling out the huge dick. Kiki slipped off the table onto the floor and in seconds she was kneeling under Sondra's cunt with her mouth firmly on it.

She didn't even bother to lick, but put her lips around the enormous hard swelling that was Sondra's clit. Then she sucked, hard, teasing it with the tip of her tongue as she did. Sondra groaned; it had been a long time since Kiki had treated her like this, and she was loving every second of it.

"Suck me!" she moaned, and Kiki did. Her finger reached back to find the tight pucker of Sondra's ass, and she slipped it in deftly. Sondra's anus was incredibly hot. The muscles held Kiki's finger like a velvet trap. She fucked Sondra's ass with her hand even as her mouth sucked her clit, and it was completed when Kiki brought up her other hand and stuck two fingers into Sondra's pussy.

Sondra felt completely filled. Kiki could feel both of her hands through the thin wall of flesh that divided the two tunnels. Both entrances were hot and wet, swollen with sex. Kiki sucked harder.

Sondra came just as noisily as Kiki did, drowned out by the music, her pleasure increased with the knowledge that other women were watching. She danced on Kiki's hands, squirmed on Kiki's mouth. It took a long time for her to finish. When she did, she pulled up her thin lover and kissed her deeply, so that she might get back the taste of her own pussyjuice on another's tongue.

Kiki had one more job to do; she slipped back to her knees to lick her nectar from the thick rubber cock. She finished just as the song finished, and she gave the huge knob at the end a kiss before she rose to change the music.

They dressed again; Kiki loved the sight of her old lover in her leathers. Once again, the crotch was packed tightly. "Where are you staying?" she asked.

"That's something I haven't even worried about yet," Sondra admitted. "I just got in a few hours ago, and visiting this bar seemed a lot more important than worrying about a pillow."

"Well," Kiki said, "I finish up around four. Got any interest in seeing what a small New York apartment looks like?"

Sondra kissed her again, a kiss that held a promise of much more to come. "I'm very interested. Just promise me that it has a double bed."

Chapter Seven

"Damn!" Ramone sighed heavily and happily. "You sure do know how to use that thing."

Sondra smiled and stroked the black cock. It was slippery with Ramone's sweet pussyjuice, for the long-haired, gray-eyed biker had just fucked her with it in the huge bed in Slash's loft, with the bar owner and her disc jockey Kiki watching intensely.

The brassy woman had been too much of a temptation for Slash and Ramone; in Sondra's own words, they thought they'd "have a piece of that." When approached, Kiki and Sondra were more than happy to oblige. Indeed, Sondra had wanted Slash from the moment she had spied her, coming to break up the commotion between the gate-crasher and the bouncer.

"It's my turn now," Slash said. She was completely nude as well, and her rich brown body shone like ebony in the half-light of the room. Sondra couldn't stop looking at her. Her body was unusual, so tall, so slim and yet muscular, completely devoid of fat, the skin as smooth as silk, the facial features razor-sharp. She looked like an artist's drawing of a woman, so perfect that she could only be rendered in pencil. Yet here she was, so real, so hot, so horny that when she bent down to Sondra's lips there was no slow kiss of introduction, but rather a hungry kiss, a starving kiss, lips pressing hard on lips and tongues pushing against each other in an orgy of oral delight.

Sondra had been lying on her side, but Slash rolled her over onto her back. The cock, strapped around her hips, stood up straight from her mound, perpetually erect. The knob was still wet from Ramone's sopping cunt.

Slash stroked it slowly, her long fingers curled around the thick rubber shaft. When her hand was completely wet from the nectar on the rubber, she put it to her mouth and slowly licked all of Ramone's sweet juice from her own skin. Sondra watched, transfixed, the cock strapped to her mound. The other two women were just as excited, and watched expectantly.

Still excruciatingly slowly, Slash straddled Sondra and positioned her cunt carefully over the large black knob. Using her fingers, she spread her pussylips and pulled them out from her body, away from the wet ruby flesh of her slit. The supple skin pulled out, and she wrapped the lips protectively around the dildo's head. She moaned softly and, to the delight of her audience, slid her cuntlips back and forth on the rubber cock while teasing the very entrance of her hole with the head.

Kiki and Ramone sat together on a chaise near the bed. As they watched, the Japanese woman put her hand between Kiki's legs and rubbed her finger up and down the superheated groove of Kiki's slit. The blue-haired woman groaned, but did not take her eyes off her friend on the bed.

The dildo was wet again now, from the juice that lubricated Slash's pussy and soaked the fleshy lips she rubbed on the head. She moved her delicious body back and forth, swaying to her own strong internal rhythm, while Sondra watched her from below. She wanted to buck her hips up and slam the cock deep into Slash's ruby cunt, but she restrained herself. It was just too much fun watching Slash dance slowly on her cock.

Just as slowly, Slash finally lowered herself onto the rubber dick. Everyone in the room sighed softly as the length of it disappeared inside her, until her pussy was resting directly on Sondra's mound. The cock was not to be seen. Her sweet asscheeks were right against the rubber balls, sandwiched between Sondra's upper thighs.

She could feel the knob right at the end of her tunnel, and she reveled in being stretched. She slithered on it, back and forth, to get the full effect. The shaft pushed hard against one side of her tunnel, and then the other, as she did.

She fucked it. She moved up and down on the shaft, taking her pussy to the very end of it and then, ever so slowly, settling back on it to swallow its hefty length completely between her cuntlips. She was putting on a show for the others as well, massaging her own flawless tits with her fingers. Sondra was doing this also and they smiled at each other. Both were sighing, their hands on their own tits, one set white with bright pink nipples, the other chocolate with brown nubs that were enlarged and hard. Joined at the pussies by a dildo that spanned both of them, they fucked slowly until Slash could take no more of the suspense, and she speeded up her motions on the rubber penis.

Sondra moaned as loudly as if the rubber cock were actually part of her body. Slash's motions pushed it against her, and she loved the feeling of being ridden, along with the wet slap of Slash's soaked pussy against her body with every deep thrust.

Slash was fucking in earnest now; she really wanted to come. She hardly noticed when Kiki got up off the lounge, didn't notice at all until she felt Sondra's legs being spread wide beneath her. She turned to see that Kiki had done this and had then slipped in between the open thighs to apply her mouth to Sondra's pussy.

Sondra writhed and squirmed on the bed with this unexpected—but very welcome—attention. She looked over at Ramone, sitting by herself on the lounge, and said, "What's the matter, are you sitting this one out?"

"Not on your life," Ramone smiled as she got up. Her pussy was hot and throbbing, just as if she hadn't come at all on the end of Sondra's cock only a short time before. As she came close to the bed, Sondra put her hand out, asking her to come closer. Within seconds, Ramone was straddled over Sondra's face, with the newcomer's tongue settled very firmly in the groove of her aching pussy.

Slash slowed for just a moment to look around and get the full effect of what was happening. She was on top of Sondra with a huge black rubber dick in her cunt. The woman she was fucking was being eaten even as she ate another with an intensity almost too strong to be believed. It was no wonder that Slash went back to fucking even faster and harder than before.

The rubber balls slapped wetly on her ass and her clit

rubbed against Sondra's mound with each thrust. Her movements pushed Sondra's pussy hard against Kiki's mouth, and the blue-haired woman flashed her tongue on the hot clit. The gold ball pierced through her tongue gave an extra thrill to Sondra's clit with each movement. Slash felt the heat and pressure in her belly and she rode hard; it had to break and push her over the edge. When it did, she screamed her pleasure.

She continued to ride the cock slowly, savoring the fullness of the rubber that distended her tunnel. Then, expertly, she turned around, so smoothly that the cock remained in her cunt even as she did. She reached down and took Kiki's head in her hands and pulled her deeper into Sondra's pussy. Kiki was surrounded by pussy; she was covered in pussy syrup; she wanted to drown in pussy. She couldn't get enough, which suited Sondra just fine. She writhed and moaned and put her cunt exactly where she wanted Kiki to lick her the hardest.

Kiki did. Sondra came explosively, bouncing so hard that Slash nearly lost her balance on her rubber perch, but Kiki's tongue never left Ramone's soaked hole. Her howls of delight were muffled by the flesh and hair stuffed into her mouth, but they were still joyfully audible to the other women. They were infectious howls, for shortly afterward, Ramone started to moan as she enjoyed her second orgasm—one that was even more spectacular than the first.

Only after Ramone's screams and shudders subsided did Slash finally get up from the rubber device that had given her so much pleasure. "Let me," Kiki said, and she inched forward on the bed to lick the dildo slowly, like an ice-cream cone, to get the delicious flavor of Slash's cunt from it. When she kissed Slash, the tall black woman took back the essence of her own body from Kiki's hot mouth. Eventually, all of them shared it in hot wet kisses that they wished could last all night.

It was a pretty interesting night at the bar. Slash had already enjoyed the sight of two women fingering each other to massive climaxes on the dance floor, a woman who put her bare tits on the bar and requested the sensual bartender to feel them up, and Sondra had come in and, to the delight of everyone near the disc jockey booth, had given her friend Kiki another go with the rubber cock that seemed almost to be a permanent part of her body.

Ramone put a hand on Slash's arm to get her attention and pointed toward the door. Slash looked up quickly and looked away. Then, her intuition telling her that something was not right, she turned around again for a longer, harder look.

The woman walking into the bar appeared as hard as nails. Her hair was shaved brutally into a brush cut, which made her rough features look even more mannish. She wore a white tank top with brand-new jeans and a worn denim jacket. Her feet were encased in heavy black jackboots. A pair of dog tags hung from a beaded metal chain around her neck.

Slash was suspicious immediately. The woman's chest was almost flat, although her nipples showed large and hard through the cotton shirt, and her walk hadn't even the hint of the steps that a woman's wider hips would cause. To top it all off, she was decidedly hairy. Her brush cut continued down her temples in downy sideburns, and there was a fringe of mustache, like an adolescent boy's, across her upper lip. Her chest was also patterned lightly with soft, downy hair, as dark as the hair on top of her head.

Slash came out from behind the bar. It was not

uncommon for cross-dressers to come into the bar, and while Slash admired them for their own particular type of sexual thrill, she also enforced the bar rule of biological women only, politely but strictly. This one, while somewhat convincing, certainly didn't appear to have been born with a cunt.

The jackbooted, denim-clad customer was now halfway across the room, heading for the bar and attracting more than her fair share of curious glances from women who watched her cross the floor.

Slash met her before she got as far as the mahogany bar. "Evening," she said.

"Hello," the stranger replied. Her voice was deep and throaty and Slash was even more convinced that her first impression had been correct.

Slash looked her up and down. If this really was a woman…Slash looked at the pattern of hair on the chest. The soft hairs pointed downward, moving across and meeting, then going down inside the tank shirt. They were sparse and soft, but they were there.

"I'm really sorry," Slash said. "But we have a policy here—dykes only. I'm afraid you'll have to leave."

To her surprise, the person before her smiled. "Don't be sorry. I get this all the time," she said, in her deep, masculine voice. "It's the hair and these little tits. But I am a dyke."

Slash stood back and sized her up again. Then, without hesitation, she reached forward and felt the woman's crotch.

The woman actually leaned into her touch and closed her eyes, moving her hips forward to press Slash's hand harder into her crotch. Still serious and businesslike, Slash felt carefully. To her surprise, she found that she had been wrong. There was no cock in those jeans.

The hairy woman grinned at her. "If we're going to be so intimate, I should tell you my name is Chris. You handled the equipment. You realize I'm going to ask that you follow up on that."

Slash looked at her evenly; now that the truth was out, she wanted to see more. "You can count on it. I have to look after a couple of things. Then I'll be back."

She went back to her post behind the bar, while Chris flagged Stef down and ordered a beer.

Ramone was waiting. "You let him stay?" she asked incredulously.

"That's no he," Slash replied.

"No shit!" Ramone exclaimed. "All that hair, and that's not a TV?"

"Not unless I've lost my sense of touch," Slash said. "I checked, and that's a pussy in those pants."

Ramone looked over. "Well, I've never seen anything like that before."

"I'm having some of it," Slash said, wiping her hands on a bar towel. "You want to see more of it, too?"

"You mind?"

"I wouldn't have invited you if I did," Slash replied. "I wouldn't have anything I wouldn't share with you in a second."

That was how they both ended up in the largest of the rooms at the back of the bar with Chris.

Chris was the center of attention, and she was loving it. She waited while Slash and Ramone stood back, and then she slid out of the denim jacket very slowly. Her arms were covered with dark hair, and her armpits were bushy. Slash and Ramone, both of them almost completely hairless, looked forward to this interesting diversion.

The white tank top was next, and when it came off, Chris stood before them with only the dog tags hanging between her breasts. Her tits were so small that they were mere bumps on her chest, more like well-developed muscles. The nipples, though, were absolutely huge.

The hair that had teased them above the shirt came together in a thin, downy line that disappeared into the waistband of her jeans. The tits themselves were hairless, the skin a rich olive color, but each luscious nipple was ringed with a circle of fine hairs that might have laid flat, but now were disheveled, standing straight up from the skin, mussed by her shirt when she took it off. Ramone longed to smooth them all down with her tongue.

The body under all of the hair was as hard as any could possibly be. This was definitely the result of long, hard, intensive workouts, and she was as thin, as firm, as muscular as Slash. The muscles of her arms were visible individually. The flesh of her belly was flat and firm. Her waist was tight above her narrow hips. This was a woman who lived for her body, and the hours she'd spent on it showed.

Her jackboots were already off her feet. Now she unzipped the jeans and slipped out of them as well. Under them she wore men's boxer shorts; Slash was surprised to see that they were silk. Chris noticed her expression. "Weren't expecting that, were you?" she asked. "Every girl needs her own luxury. They feel good when I rub them on my pussy."

She slipped them off very slowly. The cloth slid smoothly on the hair. Slash and Ramone could only stare, completely fascinated. This was indeed an unusual creature.

She had more pubic hair than the two had ever seen. It was so thick and bushy between her legs that it stood out from between her thighs, spreading at least an inch and a half away from her cunt. It lost a bit of length but none of its thickness as it moved up from her pussy to cover most of her belly. It subsided only an inch below her navel, where it came together in a point that stopped just below the whorl of her belly button. Below, it spilled out onto her inner thighs; the skin was all but invisible under the thick dressing of hair. It thinned again as it went down her legs, which were hairy right down to her ankles. Even the tops of her toes were dark with little tufts of hair.

"Incredible!" Ramone said as she looked over every inch of this amazing woman. From behind it was more of the same: a soft layer of downy dark hair adorned the skin of her back.

"It started growing when I was nine," Chris said proudly. "I shaved it all off for a while, when I was young. But then I realized what a turn-on it was for a lot of other women. It was a turn-on for me, too, and I realized I had better things to do with my time than spend it in front of a mirror shaving. Some women think I'm a freak, but I don't give a shit about them. I keep it for those who think I'm the hottest thing since sliced bread."

Slash could feel her pussy juicing up at this decidedly different type of woman. "You're the first woman I've ever seen like this," she said. "I never really thought about it. But now that I've seen it…" She didn't finish her sentence, but instead moved forward to run her hands over Chris's small tits and huge nipples.

Both she and Ramone led the hairy woman to the cot and stretched her out on it. They were captivated. They stroked the hair from her head to her feet, and Ramone reveled in all the different textures on this single body.

Her brush cut was spiky, the hair on her lip downy. Her armpit hair was straight and wiry, completely the opposite of the softer hair that made its way across her chest and between her small tits. Ramone fulfilled her desire to lick the hair around the nipple and smooth it flat. Chris sighed at the touch of her hot tongue on it and moaned even louder when Ramone took the huge nipple into her mouth and sucked hard on it.

Slash started with the other one. It was an interesting contrast, the nubby, hairless nipple surrounded by the spiky growth and she rubbed her tongue on both to get the full effect. Her hands meanwhile were moving up and down Chris's body. She felt as if she really wasn't touching the woman's flesh at all, as if her hand was held away from the skin by the covering of hair. She smoothed the downy growth between the tits, followed it down to the navel. When she reached the thick bush of Chris's mound, she plowed her hand into it and let the tufts of hair spring up between her fingers. It was almost like dipping her hand into a sheep's fleece, except that it was prickly. Closer to her cunt it was hot, with a light sheen of pussyjuice over all of it.

Slash slipped her finger into the tunnel, half-expecting it to be hairy, too. It was smooth, hot, wet, tight around her hand. Chris writhed on it and bucked her hips up until Slash put her thumb on the huge clit. It was almost impossible to find under its thick protective overcoat of hair and the swollen lips that surrounded it. When Slash touched it, Chris went wild.

Slash wanted it badly. She moved down so that her face was opposite Chris's crotch. Slash may have loved shaving Ramone, but she was equally fond of bushy cunts, and this one was the hairiest she had ever seen. She took a mouthful of the hair, sucked it in, took the cunt moisture from the strands. She pulled it between her teeth and then sucked in a mouthful again. Her hand felt for Chris's ass. The cheeks were covered with a light fuzz so delicate that it almost seemed to be a layer of her skin. The crack in between was adorned with soft hair that ran down to become part of the bushy forest that covered the entire area between her legs.

She felt she was wading into a carpet of long grass as she reached with her tongue for Chris's slit. She actually had to pull the mat of pubic hair apart with her fingers, and when she did, she stopped to admire what she saw. The hair parted evenly and uncovered a slit that seemed filled to bursting with a huge clit. The entrance to her hole was surrounded by puffy, thick lips, and the labia went down to a sweetly whorled asshole that was ringed with dark hair. Slash leaned down, pressing her tongue through the hair, and reached the nectar-soaked clit.

Chris groaned as she did and reached down to pull Slash's head closer to her. Ramone was reaching over her to suck on her nipples, and Chris lifted her head to the tits that were hanging in her face. She sucked as well, and the two sixty-nined each other's nipples as Slash ate the hairy cunt that she had wanted so badly.

Ramone slid out of her pants so expertly that Chris hardly even realized she had taken them off until she saw the Japanese woman's completely naked, shaved cunt. "Now this is something different," she said, and she indicated with movements on Ramone's thighs that she should get on top. It didn't take any more urging than that for Ramone to do so, and she straddled Chris's face while keeping her fingers on the hair-ringed nipples, kneading the small, firm breasts as she did.

Chris had never had a completely shaved cunt before, and it was as much a novelty for her as her hirsute one was for Slash. She circled all around it with her tongue just to feel skin that should be prickly but instead was as smooth as the silk shorts she had discarded. With no hair on it, the skin felt twice as hot on her tongue. She licked hard and fast, her mustache hairs quickly glued down to her upper lip with Ramone's pussyjuice.

The room was filled with the sound of their licking and the scent of rich, hot pussy. Slash put two fingers into Chris's hole and fucked her that way even as her tongue broke through the hairy bush to lick hard on her clit. In turn, Chris did the same to Ramone, perched above her head and grinding her cunt on Chris's mouth as hard as she could to get every bit of pleasure from of the touch of Chris's tongue.

It was Ramone who came first, loudly, explosively, all but spinning on Chris's tongue as she squirmed and ground. Chris stayed with her all the way, grabbing her smooth buttocks and pushing her tongue deep into the completely bare slit. Just as Ramone finished, the pressure built in Chris's belly until there was no more room for it, and out it surged. Slash's mouth filled with hot pussyjuice and hair as she came, first with a small tremor that made her shiver and then, seconds later, with an overwhelming climax that shook her right through her entire body.

They lay gasping together, the three of them, the hairless women and the one with more hair than seemed possible for a single person. As they caught their breath together, Ramone and Slash still ran their hands over Chris's body. They couldn't get enough of the unusual feeling, of the feminine cunt and breasts covered with the masculine coat of hair, so warm and smooth under their fingers.

Chris seemed equally fascinated with Ramone's hairless slit and with Slash's long, lanky, muscular body, so like her own in build but without the bearded covering. Such was the bewitchment among all three that Slash and Ramone left the bar to Stef and Cherry and came out only a few minutes before closing time, completely satisfied and all but exhausted. The two women finishing up behind the bar could only stare, openmouthed, as their bosses came out of the cubicle with what they could only assume was a hairy man in jeans.

Slash laughed at their expressions. "I know what you're thinking," she said as she put an arm around Chris's neck and kissed her cheek. "Your old friend hasn't gone bi on you. Let's just say it's been one hairy night."

Chapter Eight

"That looks like someone we could work with," Cherry said. "What do you think?"

Stef nodded her head slowly. "You have radar for them, I swear," she said in awe. "You're definitely right about this one."

The two waitresses, enjoying a well-earned break together, stared across the room at the woman who had caught their attention. She was a petite woman, nicely built, with shoulder-length brown hair that was tied back in a ponytail. She wore tight-fitting jeans and a plain T-shirt that showed off perky medium-sized breasts. The sexual tension she felt was evident in the nipples that bulged through the thin fabric of the shirt and the way she almost unconsciously squirmed on the hard chair to put pressure on her pussy.

She was sitting at a small table, all by herself, and was

watching a couple at the next table unashamedly. She was so enthralled by it that she undoubtedly didn't realize she was staring so intently. It was this wonder, along with her expression, that caught Cherry's eye immediately. This woman was a virgin and, judging by what she was watching, she was a most intriguing candidate for Cherry's smooth delivery and possible later deflowering.

Actually, only one woman was sitting at the next table, and she was regal indeed in her chair. She wore a heavy leather jacket with a black leather corset under it, fishnet stockings, and shiny black boots that came right up to her thighs. Her hands were encased in fingerless leather gloves, buckled across the backs, that showed off long fingers and perfect nails done in flawless crimson polish. She wore makeup—a lot of it—dark around her eyes, done so expertly that she looked like a sultry movie star. She had turned a few heads when she had come into the bar and was continuing to do so from her seat.

The woman beside her was definitely not in the same category. She wore cutoff jeans and a halter top that left her back bare. Her skin was dark in stripes with old bruises that were healing slowly. There was a chain about one bare ankle—not a gold one for decoration, but solid chrome links with a ring that could have a shackle snapped to it at any time. Similar chrome chains bound her thin wrists.

A black leather dog collar was around her throat, and a leash was attached to it, the other end looped casually around her Mistress's arm. This submissive sat directly on the floor, beside the chair where her leather-clad Mistress sat. There were two drinks on the table, and the haughty woman sipped at one. Occasionally she would take the other and feed it to her submissive, as if to a child, allowing her a small sip, wiping her chin with a napkin, and then putting the glass back on the table until it pleased her to hand it down again.

It was this scene that the long-haired woman was watching, with a yearning in her eyes that was almost an ache. Stef and Cherry sized her up immediately. Not only was she a virgin, but it wasn't the Mistress with whom she was so taken. There was admiration for that regal woman, of course, but the longing, the hungry craving, was definitely for the position of the dog-collared submissive on the floor.

"You in or out?" Cherry asked.

Stef laughed. "What do you think?"

Cherry got up and walked over to the bar. "Need us for a little while?" she asked Slash.

Slash looked over. "What are you two working on now?"

"Over there, by herself," Cherry said and waited while Slash sized up the woman who was so fascinated by the dominatrix and her slave. "What do you think?"

"I think," Slash said lightheartedly, "that you find far more than your fair share of virgins before the rest of us get a chance to see them. Hey, I wouldn't turn it down. Take all the time you need."

"The stuff still there?"

Slash bent down behind the bar and came back up with a small leather duffel bag, which she passed over. "Let me know how it goes," she said.

The duffel could easily double as a purse, and this was how Cherry carried it as she made her way back to the petite woman who was still engrossed with the couple at the next table. Stef watched her. She was unable to hear what they said, but Cherry's meaning and the young woman's reactions were unmistakable. Once again Stef was awestruck by Cherry's singular ability to convince any virgin she chose that getting up and following her to the back of the bar was the only thing that virgin had ever wanted. In less than ten minutes, the young woman was on her feet, following Cherry as she carried the leather duffel bag and made her way through the crowd.

Stef was waiting for them. "This is Cory," Cherry explained. Cory held out her hand in greeting, but Stef ignored her. After a few seconds, Cory dropped her arm, unsure whether to be upset or angry. You'll understand soon enough, Stef thought, and out of the corner of her eye she sized up the virgin Cherry had brought to her. She looked as good close up as she had at a distance; the tits were firm, the nipples were still visible through the T-shirt, the ass in the tight jeans looked nicely rounded. This was definitely something they could work with.

"Coming with us?" Cherry asked as Stef continued to stand there.

They both heard a gasp from Cory, and they turned to see her looking at them, first one, then the other. It was obvious from her expression that she wasn't anticipating her first time to be witnessed by a second woman, and she looked confused and shy.

Cherry sized up the situation immediately. When she spoke, she was firm but polite, businesslike but almost kind. "I know you weren't expecting this, but there are going to be two of us," she said. "A lot of women like you would think they'd died and gone to heaven, but you don't know a lot about that yet.

"We're only into consent; we don't do it any other way. If you don't want this, that's fine. Just say so now, and that will be the end of it, no hard feelings. But if you want to try this, you'll try it with both of us. What will it be?"

Cory looked at both of them again, thought for a moment, breathed deeply, and then looked at Cherry firmly. "I've wanted this all my life. Yes, it's fine with me."

They continued walking, Cory a step behind. Cherry and Stef exchanged smiles. Little did Cory know that it would be the last time she would look so evenly into a Mistress's eye! And little did she know that she was following two of the cruelest Mistresses any submissive had ever bowed before. She did not realize the looks that a couple of them gave to the threesome as they passed, looks from women who had crept on their hands and knees, and loved every second of it, before Cherry, or Stef, or both. Had Cory only known it, the envy in their eyes would have told her that she could be in for the ride of her life.

The door to the largest domination cubicle was open, and Stef and Cherry stopped at the threshold and indicated that Cory go ahead of them. Then they watched her expectantly as she entered the room and checked out her surroundings.

Cory looked around with a sense of wonder. They could see in her eyes that this was the day she had always dreamed about, and now that it was really here, she almost couldn't believe it. Nearly in a daze, she looked at the table, its heavy top scarred from so many years of chains shackled across it and whips snapped on it for the sheer pleasure of the sound of leather smacking against it. She looked at the rings set into the wall at their various heights, imagining how difficult and uncomfortable it would be to have one's hands shackled to the rings right at the ceiling. She was green, though, and didn't know that Stef's favorite position was to attach her charges to the highest rings by the cuffs on their feet.

Then the two dominatrixes entered the room as well and closed the door behind them. Cherry put the black leather duffel bag on the table. "I'm going to ask once more," she said. "Are you sure?"

There was no hesitation in Cory's voice now. "Absolutely."

The Mistresses were all business. "Then there is no excuse for your behavior at this point," Cherry said. "We are your superiors; you are nothing but worthless scum here for our amusement. From now on you will obey our rules implicitly. You will not speak unless spoken to, or unless you beg permission and we decide to grant it. You will do nothing unless you are ordered to do so. You will address us as 'Mistress'—if you need to be specific, I am Mistress Cherry, and this is Mistress Stef. We will tolerate absolutely no deviation from these rules. Have I made myself completely clear?"

"Yes," Cory said, and then added "Mistress" quickly. Cherry and Stef nodded to each other. This was going to be a wonderful deflowering.

"I believe you are wearing too much," Stef said. "You will now undress completely."

This seemed to catch Cory off guard, as if somehow she had not been expecting to perform before these women naked. It was enough for Stef. Before Cory could even see her, she pulled back her arm and smacked the young woman fiercely across the face with her open hand.

Cory gasped, more shocked than anything, and her own hand flew to her injured cheek. "Put it down!" Stef ordered. This time, Cory obeyed. The Mistresses admired the red blotch on her skin where the blow had landed.

"Now," Stef said firmly, "I still believe you are wearing too much."

A second slap wasn't necessary; Cory peeled off her shirt and slipped out of her jeans, repeating "Yes, Mistress," as she did, following a warning by Cherry that such a reply was always necessary following a command. Now that the first blow had fallen and Cory had found that this was all very real, they were certain that she would not forget soon.

They both looked her over, coldly, as if she were a piece of meat, and their expressions were not lost on Cory. She felt worthless at this point, felt like nothing more than a toy for their amusement, inconsequential, necessary to them only as a plaything to vent their cruelty upon. She realized then that any submissive woman would do for them, that her individual qualities were of little concern. This was not entirely true, of course, for both of the Mistresses were thoroughly enjoying the fact that they were putting this woman through her submissive paces for the first time ever. Aside from that, however, Cory's impressions were correct.

Their cool glances, plus the fact that they were clothed while she was naked, made her feel more vulnerable than she ever had in her life, and for a brief moment she wanted to cover herself. She wanted to fold her arms across her breasts, cup a hand protectively over her naked pussy. She forced herself to keep her arms at her side. For a moment it was fear; she dreaded another rough slap across her face. But then it was as if a light had gone on inside her head. She kept her arms at her sides because her Mistresses would not like her to cover herself up—and she suddenly realized that she wanted desperately to please these two women. Suddenly her expression was so different that Stef and Cherry looked at each other and their pussies began to throb. There was nothing finer than the look on a submissive's face when she realized that the whole concept was not just pain and suffering, but a desire, a need, an insatiable craving to obey and please her Mistress.

Now the leather duffel was opened, and Cherry reached inside. "Put out your wrists," she ordered.

"Yes, Mistress," the novice replied, and she held them up. Almost instinctively, she did it palm-up, in the traditional gesture of submission; Stef wondered if she had done her homework with B&D movies or if perhaps it was just a natural reaction for someone who needed to be dominated. She also kept her eyes down; her even glance at Cherry when being asked for consent had been the last time she had looked either Mistress in the face.

Cherry had taken a pair of leather cuffs out of the bag. She handed one to Stef, and they slipped them over Cory's wrists, each one buckling one of the shackles. Cory sighed happily. After all her years of dreaming, she was discovering that the reality was turning out to be just as good as the anticipation.

The cuffs had rings on them, and Cherry attached a snap that bound their captive's wrists to each other. Now, for the first time, Cory was helpless. They noticed that she pulled her wrists apart, ever so slightly, slowly, so that they might not notice. They did not punish her, but watched her carefully. She was reveling in the fact that she was now under their control and that she could not possibly separate her hands even if she wanted to. Her small breasts rose and fell beautifully as she sighed happily, and they also noted that her nipples were huge and hard. Cherry knew that if she were to place a hand between those thighs, she would find the brown pussy-hair soaked with hot juice from her hole.

This was too much for Cherry, whose own pussy was

hot with anticipation. She wanted to be cruel, so she grabbed Cory's arms, spun her around, and flung her on her stomach over the table.

Taken by surprise, Cory gasped, but she did not move. Instead, she stretched limply across the table, ready for anything her Mistresses might do to her. It was uncomfortable for her; she was bent over at the waist, her tits mashed against the wooden tabletop. Her discomfort only added to her joy at being under the control of these women.

"What do you think?" Cherry asked as she sized up Cory from behind.

"I like it," Stef said. It was indeed nice. Cory's buttocks were silky smooth, pale, sweetly rounded. They were begging for a Mistress's touch, and indeed, Cory was, too. The Mistresses could see her slit from this angle and, as Cherry had anticipated, it was soaking wet with sexual excitement. There was no doubt that this virgin was enjoying everything that was being done to her.

Cherry took a short chain from the duffel bag. She wanted this virgin to know that she meant business. The end of the chain was attached to the snap that fastened the cuffs together. It was looped around the leg of the table and then brought back up, over the tabletop, and the other end snapped firmly. Now Cory was completely in their control, lashed to the tabletop, unable to lift herself up. Both Mistress and submissive were satisfied with the arrangement: Cherry because she loved the sight of a helpless woman chained down, and Cory because, for the first time, she was the woman she had so admired in all those movies and pictures—the slave who was chained, the slave who was helpless under the domination of another.

Stef struck first. She came up alongside the prone slave, raised her arm, and smashed her open palm down on Cory's ass.

Cory inhaled sharply. Not only had the blow taken her by surprise, but it hurt; Stef was very strong. She hardly had time to catch her breath when Stef spanked her again, even harder, on her other asscheek.

"Would you like to have a go?" Stef asked.

"Why not both of us?" Cherry said.

"Why not!"

The Mistresses stood on either side of their captive while Cory held her breath, hardly daring to believe that she had balked at the idea of two women in the room with her—it was a dream come true. Her asscheeks were still stinging, the skin red from the blows she had already received. She quickly discovered that this was only a taste of things yet to come.

Each Mistress took an asscheek and began to spank. Cory groaned; she could hardly believe how much it hurt. She hadn't been spanked since she was a child; but, to her delight, she found that the stinging and burning of her buttocks was turning her on. The slaps fell, one after the other, sometimes simultaneously. Again and again the Mistresses struck until the room rang with the sound of their blows. It was magnificent, and the two Mistresses reveled in the punishment just as much as Cory did.

In the end, it proved too much. Just as she had when she was a child, Cory tried to put on a brave front and bit her lip. These two women were experts at domination, however, and before long, tears were streaming down Cory's face. Still she bit her lip until Cherry struck a particularly hard blow on the sensitive skin of her upper thighs. A sob broke from Cory's throat, followed by another. She could not control her weeping.

"Please!" she begged. "Please, Mistress!" She remembered a scene she had watched in a movie and thought it might work. "Please, Mistress, have mercy on me!"

Unseen by their captive, Stef and Cherry shared triumphant smiles over the red buttocks they were slapping. It would not do to answer a slave's pleas right away, of course, so each landed another four blows on the battered asscheeks before standing back. Breathing heavily from their exertion, they admired their work.

Cory's buttocks were no longer pale and silky. They were rough and raw, the skin a bright red where the blows had fallen. Her body shook with the intensity of her sobs; but to their pleasure, they saw that she had not made any attempt to move from the position she had been thrown into. There was still some slack in the chain that bound her to the table. The raw material was there. With training, this was going to prove to be a very fine slave for some Mistress.

"Why are you crying?" Cherry demanded sharply. She winked at Stef; they were thoroughly enjoying themselves.

"Please, Mistress!" Cory sobbed. The dominatrixes noticed that now the proper address slipped as easily off her tongue as if she had been doing this for years. "Please forgive me, but it hurts very much."

"So you don't want us to do this?"

Cory sobbed louder, and Stef realized it was because she feared the two women were going to end everything right there. "I do, Mistress, I do!" she said. "I didn't want to cry, I really didn't, but I couldn't help it."

"So you want more?"

Cory hesitated for just a second. She wanted to be dominated, but her ass was incredibly painful. Then she realized that complete submission meant accepting anything her Mistresses doled out to her. Cherry and Stef felt their pussies twinge with pleasure when she replied, "I want whatever my Mistresses feel like doing to me."

"A very good answer, slave," Stef said, and although she couldn't see their captive's face, she knew that there would be a smile on those lips, a self-satisfied smile that they would allow her this time. There would be plenty of time in the future for her to learn that slaves were simply not permitted the luxury of self-pride. "Mistress Cherry, what do you feel like doing?"

Mistress Cherry knew exactly; it was what she had been craving all night. She reached into the bag and pulled out one of her favorite toys, a leather-faced, wooden-handled paddle.

It wasn't the one she really wanted to use; that one was a nasty one with a thick paddle that was covered with hideously pointed chrome studs. That would come later; it was much too cruel for a virgin. This one was lighter, softer, more flexible, but that did not make it any less of a fierce weapon. While it did not have the sheer brutality of the studded paddle, in the hands of a good Mistress it could have even the hardiest and most experienced of slaves in tears, begging for mercy.

Cherry walked around to the other side of the table; having discovered her calling and already knowing a few of the rules that went with it, Cory kept her eyes at the level of Cherry's waist. "Look up here," Cherry ordered. Cory did. "Do you know what this is?"

Cory shivered; she had certainly seen enough of them, in films, in magazines, behind the counters of the leather shops she went into so reverently. "Yes, Mistress," she whispered.

"Do you know what I am going to do with it?"

"I do, Mistress." Her voice was a combination of dread and all-out sexual pleasure.

With that, Cherry walked around to the back of the table again. As she did, she ran the edge of the leather paddle lightly down Cory's spine. She smiled cruelly as she watched the young submissive shiver and arch her back at the touch. These creatures were so low! They were so basic that they could not even control their sexual desires. The merest touch could sweep them into a frenzy that they were unable to conceal. How unlike Mistresses, those superior beings who could revel in their throbbing pussies, enjoy their sex-enlarged nipples, and even experience heart-stopping orgasms without the slightest indication, should they choose to keep their satisfaction a secret.

As Cherry reached Cory's ass, Stef roughly pulled the captive's legs apart. The girl's pussy was completely soaked, a condition that the Mistresses used to their advantage.

"Look at that!" Cherry laughed. "It looks like a geyser! I told you these slaves could never keep a secret from their Mistresses."

Stef said sarcastically, "I think it's funny that they even bother juicing up at all. What do they think, that they're going to be allowed to come? Idiots! They might as well put on a parachute and never get into a plane." As they laughed, they saw that Cory's humiliation was overwhelming; although they could not see her face, her neck and even the skin of her upper back flushed brilliant scarlet with embarrassment.

Cherry decided to add frustration to her prisoner's troubles. Using the edge of the paddle, she brushed Cory's wet pussylips lightly. The young woman squirmed on the table, holding her cunt up almost involuntarily, begging for another touch. She moved so much that the chain pulled tight, forcing her wrists down on the table.

The Mistresses laughed again and made a game of it. Cherry used the thin paddle edge to part Cory's pussylips. The entrance to her tunnel was sex-swollen and ruby-red, the flesh shiny with juice. Her clit was enlarged, begging for a touch. Cherry danced the paddle edge over it several times, and Cory groaned loudly. It must have been the touch she was dying for, for she bucked her hips up and, as best she could in her position, tried to press her clit against the paddle herself. Cherry allowed her a few more feathery brushes with the leather, which was now shiny and wet on its edge with the thick, hot juice of Cory's cunt. Then the red-haired Mistress withdrew the paddle completely and used her open hand to deliver another hard blow on Cory's bruised buttocks.

The young woman moaned loudly, but not with passion. This was a groan of despair. She twitched involuntarily, confused by all the signals her body was sending her. She was excited by the touch of the paddle, frustrated by its being taken away. She was thrilled by the sexual buildup in her cunt and cramped and uncomfortable at being stretched across the table, bent at the hips, her wrists shackled and helpless. Most of all, it was that spanking across her asscheeks. It hurt, it stung, it burned on the flesh that had already been battered by both of the Mistresses' strong hands. But it excited her. It filled her with a tension dancing on the fine line between pleasure and pain, moving from one side to the other until both emotions blurred into a single reaction that filled her with the knowledge that this was what her life was meant to be. She was a submissive! She was a slave! And, from this moment on, the only thing that would have sexual meaning for her would be helplessness at a Mistress's leather-clad, stiletto-heeled feet.

Cherry and Stef realized this and decided to capitalize on it.

Cherry ran the paddle across the burning hot skin of

Cory's buttocks one more time. Then she laid the leather device across them. "If that falls off," she warned their captive, "you will not expect any quarter from us during your punishment." Then she turned to her friend, opened her own shirt, and offered her delicious breasts, one with its ring and exquisite tattoo, for a caress.

Cory was both shocked and confused. How could they ignore her, lying on the table with her arms bound and her ass bruised, and concentrate on each other? And just what were they doing? She couldn't see them, and although she desperately wanted to, she didn't dare turn her head to watch. She could only hear them, hear their sighs and low moans; for while a Mistress would never allow a slave's touch to be seen as delightful, the attentions of another dominatrix were an entirely different matter. Another dominatrix's hands on her tits, a tongue on her clit, were reasons to moan one's pleasure aloud.

Stef's tits were now uncovered as well, and the two felt each other's breasts as they kissed, long, luscious kisses with their tongues meeting and pressing against each other. When Cherry opened her jeans, Stef's hand was inside in a second, rubbing the hot flesh with fingers that couldn't wait to get to the clit and press far into the tunnel.

They were engrossed in each other, touching and prodding, kissing deeply, when their attention was taken away by a clattering sound. They turned, and at the same moment, they heard Cory catch her breath in a way that indicated knowledge of the predicament she now found herself in.

Horny beyond belief, almost overcome by the throbbing of her clit and the pressure in her belly, Cory had closed her legs slowly, hoping against hope that the Mistresses wouldn't notice the change in her position.

Once they were closed, she squeezed her thighs together tightly, pinching her clit and sending deliciously warm chills throughout her entire body.

Unfortunately, when she did, her buttocks moved, and the leather paddle slipped on her skin and fell to the tabletop.

She froze as the two women spun around and sized up the situation instantly. Cory opened her mouth to beg forgiveness, but Stef was faster.

She picked up the paddle by its leather handle and raised her arm. Before Cory could say a word, the paddle came down on her already-battered buttocks.

The Mistresses loved the sound of her scream. The spanking had been bad, but this was a hundred times worse. Again and again the paddle came up and fell, with the harsh slap that only leather against bare submissive skin can produce. The blood rose in Cory's veins, dark red right under the skin, and when Stef was done with ten blows on each side, with two blows to the small of her back and one across the top of each thigh, Cory was crying in agony again, the tears streaming down her cheeks, and all of her skin mottled deep purple where the leather had extracted its horrible punishment.

Then Stef moved to the front of the table, where Cory was trying her hardest to control her sobs. Stef thrust the paddle in front of her face. "Kiss it!" she hissed. "Kiss it, you miserable scum. Thank it for the punishment it gave you. Thank it for teaching you a valuable lesson in obedience!"

Cory did, her tears falling on the black leather paddle. She could hardly believe herself. Just a little while before, all of this had just been a fantasy, something she'd wanted all her life but never thought for an instant she'd ever experience. Now here she was, cuffed, beaten, thanking the paddle that had done such damage to her asscheeks that she didn't think she'd be able to sit comfortably for a week.

The subtlety of her new role, all of the details, the mind games that dominatrixes played so well were ahead of her, and she knew this. She knew she had a lot to learn. But she also knew that today's lessons had already sunk in. She realized that submission meant pain; it meant doing things that she normally wouldn't even consider doing. But if pain and humiliation pleased a Mistress, then she would be first in line when they were handed out!

All of the magazines, all of the movies had shown her the basics of what she was now into. She had known the movements, the Mistresses' commands, the submissive's response, the punishments long before Mistress Stef and Mistress Cherry had brought her in here and lashed her to the table. Now she glowed with the realization that she had begun her inner journey into the intricacies, the motivations, the needs and cravings that brought Mistress and slave together for mutual satisfaction.

She was brought out of her reverie by Cherry, who unchained her arms and took off the fastener that held her wrist cuffs together. "You will go back into the bar," she said and motioned Cory to stand up.

"Yes, Mistress," the slave replied. It was almost impossible for her to get up. Her muscles were cramped from leaning over for so long, and her asscheeks burned freshly as she moved. Her cunt was still hot and wet, longing for sexual release that would never come for her. She stumbled a little; it took a few moments before she could stand. Then she reached for the clothes she had dropped.

"Oh, no," Cherry said. "You're going out like that."

Cory turned. Her eyes opened wide in horror. Before she could speak, though, Cherry said coldly, "Make up your mind right this second. You can put on those clothes, go out there, and throw away everything we've taught you tonight. Or you can obey us, like the slave that we know you are." Without a second thought, Cory straightened up and left the clothes behind.

"You will sit at the table where we found you," Stef said. "You will wait for us until we come for you."

"But Mistress," Cory pleaded, "the bar is crowded. I'm sure there's someone sitting there now."

"Then you will have to make her leave," Stef said. "We will come for you, I won't say how long from now. If you're not sitting in that chair, completely naked, with those cuffs on your wrists, we'll make you wish you had never been born."

"Yes, Mistress," Cory replied. She did not look forward to the scene she would have to make in the bar—what if, she thought in absolute, bone-chilling horror, the woman now in her chair was a Mistress? But this Mistress had ordered it, and she would have to obey. At a gesture from Cherry, she turned and opened the door. She breathed deeply, taking just a second to summon her courage. Then she slipped out into the crowd.

She wasn't gone a second when Cherry slipped out of her jeans. Her cunt rings gleamed gold in the light as she slid onto the table. She opened her legs wide; her own slit was wet with want.

"What do you say?" she asked. "I'm going to leave that little bitch out there for quite a while. In the meantime, I think it's only fair that these Mistresses should have some fun of their own."

Stef bent down to put her mouth at the level of the cunt she had wanted to lick all night. "I say we should let the fun begin."

Chapter Nine

"Got your ticket?" the burly bouncer growled to the next person in line.

"Right here"—and another woman was admitted into the velvety darkness of Rough Trade.

Slash walked among the capacity crowd, admired by everyone she passed, and basked in the hot sexual tension that was building up in the bar. She had been advertising this evening's entertainment for weeks, and interest was so high that she had had tickets printed up, distributed free of charge on a first-come, first-served basis. She had hired extra security for the front door and told them the strict rules of no entry without a ticket. She feared that otherwise, leaving the doors wide open as she did every other night might result in a riot when the place overfilled. As it was, the tickets were gone in the first week. She found herself having to turn down telephone requests from dykes two states away. While Slash had given the tickets out free, it was rumored that there was a thriving black market where the pasteboard slips were going for as high as $1,000 each.

Slash didn't know whether or not to believe it, but she certainly didn't discourage the rumors. She remembered the first night the bar was open, before anyone had heard of Rough Trade, when she had served up a whole six glasses of beer the entire night to three lonely dykes who drank up and then headed out for a livelier bar down the street. Now that bar was closed for lack of business, and Rough Trade never had a single night when there wasn't a lineup outside the door of butches, femmes, dominatrixes, slaves, lipsticks, curious thrill-seekers and experienced dykes waiting for their turn to step inside.

"Slash! Is this going to be everything you promised?" a woman called out from across the floor.

Slash turned; she recognized the huge-breasted woman immediately, a regular who came in almost every night. "Have I ever delivered less than I've promised?" she asked.

The reply was an approving look up and down the lanky bar owner's body. "If it's half as hot as you, Slash, I'll be grabbing any sweet young thing I can find, 'cause I'll need my pussy licked just so I can stay calm enough to watch," the woman laughed.

It was true; Slash had seldom looked hotter. She wore a skintight red leather corset that ended just below her breasts, the wire support cups pushing her tits up so that the nipples stood straight out. The leather that went between her legs was a thin strap, just barely enough to cover her slit, with her tightly curled pubic hair spreading out on both sides of it. Leather garters held up red stockings, and her feet were thrust into soft red leather boots. Their high, thin heels increased her already-excessive height. No matter where one stood in the bar, Slash was visible above the crowd.

She walked over to the dance floor, which had been cordoned off for the evening to keep it empty. She was watched closely by women in the crowd as she did. Although the music was loud, the sound of her heels snapped out on the hardwood floor.

There was a huge ring set deep into the ceiling and from it hung a length of thick, heavy metal chain, also ending in a ring. Hooked to it was a leather harness.

Slash pulled the harness apart, admiring it, knowing that the women ringing the dance floor wanted to feel it on their fingers also. The leather straps were thick, heavy, black, with that unmistakable musty animal smell. The straps were joined by chrome rings and bright rivets. The outer sides of the straps were finished smoothly, tanned and burnished, but the insides were unfinished and rough.

The harness consisted of two lengths that ended in wide loops, for a woman's legs to be thrust into, the straps holding her under her thighs. Loops farther up on the lengths were for her wrists. A single strap joined both lengths together, made to cradle her back. Once a woman was inside the harness, she was helpless, hanging above the floor in a sitting position. Her pussy would be exposed and vulnerable, easily accessible from below. The loops that held her thighs and wrists were loose now, but they had buckles on the end of them so that if necessary, they could be tightened firmly around her limbs and fastened securely. The harness had a dual purpose. It could be used gently, lovingly, between two women who wanted to use it to explore; or it could be cruel, nasty, a fitting punishment for a slave in need of heavy discipline.

For this evening's entertainment, its occupant would be consenting, looking forward to it. Slash enjoyed such scenes. But it also wasn't out of character for the bar's patrons for someone who hadn't expected such a device to be part of her evening's agenda to come forward—or be brought forward.

She looked at her watch, then over at Ramone behind the bar, and nodded. Ramone nodded in return, served up the drink she had been pouring, and left the bar in Stef's hands. Slash watched as her friend, clad in tight jeans and an equally tight T-shirt, walked through the crowd and climbed the staircase that wound its way up to Slash's loft.

Slash went back to the bar to help serve the capacity crowd.

At the stroke of ten, having gone upstairs to change her clothes, she signaled to Kiki, who turned off the loud, pounding music. The buzz of voices was now the only sound in the bar; but with the music off, everyone became quiet. It was an eerie feeling, the entire bar filled shoulder to shoulder with women, all of them silent. Slash's heels clicking on the floor seemed to be the only sound in the entire room as she walked to the center of the bar.

A spotlight was on the floor, illuminating the harness, which looked even more sinister as it hung suspended from the ceiling. The chrome chains and rings glinted blindingly in the light while the leather looked even blacker. The light also glinted off a large glass jar that sat on the floor near where the harness hung. Submissives all around the room shivered, many of them knowing the feeling of those loops buckled tightly around their legs as they hung at their Mistress's mercy; dominatrixes smiled coldly, some imagining how intriguing such a device would look in their torture chambers, others reminded of scenes with similar devices they had had with their slaves.

Even women who weren't into such nasty roles still looked on with considerable interest, thinking of their girlfriends hung up with their pussies available to fingers and tongues, or imagining themselves hanging gently in the loops with their lovers near them to take advantage of the position.

"You've all come for this tonight," Slash told her audience, and then waited while the crowd cheered, long and loud, taking several minutes before they quieted down. "Let's get this show on the road!"

Kiki started up her music, and Slash looked off to her side. From deep within the crowd, Ramone came forward.

She was magnificent. Her body was accentuated by leather that was as dark and shiny as the straps that made up the harness. She wore a close-cropped sleeveless leather vest, open at the front, with nothing under it save her rich olive skin and deliciously firm breasts. Her legs were covered with leather chaps, starting at a belt that was fastened around her hips. Her dark pussy and her sweetly rounded buttocks were uncovered as well, and her feet were thrust into heavy black motorcycle boots with straps that circled her ankles. The crowd cheered again.

Now a second woman came out from the crowd. Marya was an old friend of Ramone's. She was a petite woman, small-boned, with tiny ankles and wrists. Her features were boyish, her hair to her shoulders in back, but cut in wisps around her face; decidedly feminine gold earrings softened her look. She was wearing a marvelously ornate Japanese kimono, and her feet were bare, a thin gold chain about one ankle.

When she got to the middle of the floor, under the hot light, she slipped off the kimono. Her body was delicious. She was lithe; fit, but not overly muscular; dainty, but with obvious strength. Her breasts were small, beautifully nippled. Her pussy was delicate as well, the hair of her mound shaved neatly into a circle, the slit itself completely hairless. There was no stubble there; it had been shaved clean earlier that day, in Slash's loft, with the straight razor.

She greeted Ramone with a long, passionate kiss that raised another cheer from the tightly packed audience. Slash looked around in amazement, suddenly realizing just how full the bar really was, now that everyone's attention was focused on the same thing. Up front, women jostled for a position to see better; in behind, they stood on tables and chairs, not wanting to miss an instant of the entertainment spectacle Slash had promised.

Ramone stood back, grinned, and then reached for her friend. Marya threw her head back in delight as Ramone's fingers found her nipples and played with them. Ramone pulled them out, away from Marya's body, stretching the skin. Marya groaned aloud and put her own hand between her legs to touch her sex-swollen clit.

She climbed into the harness easily. The bottom loops went loosely around her thighs, and she slid her arms into the top straps and leaned back into the leather sling that supported her back. She fit into it as if it had been made for her. The harness swung with the effort, and she moved back and forth in midair. The women at the very edge of the circle around her had to suppress an urge to run forward, bend over, and put their tongues into the cunt placed there so conveniently.

That cunt was indeed accessible. As Marya hung in the harness, her pussy was just at the height of Ramone's shoulder. Ramone reached up and ran one finger along the length of Marya's slit, which was already well soaked with juice. Marya groaned, and a collective sigh went up from the entire bar. Everyone there could imagine Ramone's finger on her slit, teasing her clit, moving across her tunnel's opening, stopping for just a moment on the rosebud of her ass.

Marya's ass was the center of attraction now. From one pocket of her vest, Ramone pulled a small pale pink buttplug, which she showed all around to the audience. She licked it several times to wet it, and then she reached to put the very end of it against the whorl of Marya's asshole.

She pushed the plug in as slowly as she possibly could, and Marya moaned. She loved having her ass filled. The cone-shaped plug opened her sphincter gradually and entered just a little farther into her hot, velvety tunnel as Ramone pressed. Wider and wider it opened her, until she was dilated so much, the sensation almost passed the level of pleasure and moved into pain. Just before it did, Ramone pushed it in right to the small rubber collar. The muscular ring seized tight around it, and Marya sighed happily at the deliciously full feeling.

Now, from another pocket, Ramone took a medium-sized dildo. This one was just a thick rubber rod, smooth at the tip, not meant to look like a penis at all. It was a toy for a woman to give to another woman, a gift of total lesbian femininity.

She took the tip of the rod and ran it up and down

Marya's slit just as she had her hand, several times. It quickly became coated with the thick juice flowing so copiously from Marya's hole that it filled the trough of her cunt like a well. Ramone licked the hot fluid from it, savoring the winy taste, before she put the tip of the rod to the edge of Marya's tunnel and inserted it.

She moved just as slowly as she had with the buttplug. Marya, who could have happily spent twenty-four hours of each day with both of her holes filled, swung herself in the harness joyfully just so the dildo would press hard against the walls of her cunt-tunnel. The crowd cheered as the entire length of the rubber rod disappeared, but then they began to stomp their feet and whistle. This was nice, but it wasn't what they had come to see.

Ramone decided the time was right for that. She pulled the rod out of Marya's hole and wiped it clean on her own tits, so that they shone with her hot secretions in the white light. Now she reached down, to the glass jar that sat on the floor, and slowly, teasing the whole room, she picked it up and unscrewed the lid.

It was filled with grease. She scooped out a handful, put the jar down, and held out her right arm.

Maddeningly slowly, she lubricated her hand and arm with a thick coating. It was resembled axle grease, the same consistency, a light caramel color. It was thick grease, meaty grease, and when she was finished, Ramone held her fist in the air to the crowd's deafening cheers. The grease gleamed gold in the light.

Keeping a tight, solid fist, she placed her hand on Marya's cunt.

It seemed impossible that any woman as small as Marya would be able to take such a thing. Indeed, she sucked in her breath as Ramone's fist first spread her cuntlips, leaving thick gobs of grease on the hairless lips.

But she held her breath because it felt so good, and she moaned aloud as Ramone's knuckles disappeared between the fleshy lips, into the heat of her tunnel.

She pressed as smoothly and slowly as she had with the buttplug and the rubber rod. The whole room held its breath as the widest part of Ramone's fist, where the knuckle of her thumb stuck out, reached the entrance. It slipped inside, smoothed by the thick lubricant, and Marya moaned. "Give me more, Ramone!" she said throatily. "I can take it all, girl. Give it to me, please!"

Ramone did. Her entire fist disappeared; she was now in up to her wrist. Still she gave Marya more—and still more—until Cherry, standing beside Slash, exclaimed in awe, "She's up to her fucking elbow!"

She almost was. Her whole fist and half of her arm was now inside Marya, swinging joyfully in the harness. "That's it, Ramone!" she said. "Fuck me with it. Fist-fuck me, girl—you know how much I love it!"

Ramone fucked her slowly, but Marya, hot and sweaty, horny and needy, wanted much more than that. She held the leather straps as if on a child's swing and bounced in the loops to bring her pussy up and down on Ramone's fist. Eager to give her friend just what she wanted, Ramone fucked her faster. They met at the end of each stroke, Marya's pussy bearing down hard as Ramone brought her fist up to meet her.

Ramone thrust upward. Her whole arm was hot. She could feel the velvety, muscular walls of Marya's tunnel sucking on her fist to draw her in. She could feel the buttplug through the division between Marya's canals. Almost unconsciously, her other hand was between her own legs, feeling her own pussy. She slipped two fingers inside her own; it was as hot and wet as Marya's, and just as needy.

Pussyjuice was running down her arm, gleaming wet on top of the grease on Ramone's arm. It puddled in the crook of her elbow. "Fuck me harder!" Marya moaned, to a collective sigh from the crowd. Half the women in the audience wanted to have a fist up Marya's expansive pussy; the other half wanted to be hanging there, with Ramone's arm in her cunt.

"Fist her! Fist her!" It was a chant the crowd took up, and soon everyone was repeating it, stomping their feet and clapping. "Fist her! Fuck her!" Ramone smiled. She took up the rhythm with them. She thrust her fist deep into Marya's tunnel, right to the end of it, until she could feel the hot membranes hold her back. She pulled out, almost all the way, until her knuckles were the only thing holding Marya's vagina open. Then she pumped back in, while Marya groaned and arched her back, her eyes closed, her mouth open in ecstasy.

She came ferociously. She growled and screamed, moaned, tried to pound on Ramone's fist as hard as she could. Her nipples stood out almost straight. Her body was bathed in sweat, her chest flushed and hot. She trembled convulsively as the orgasm ripped through her. When it was over, she slumped limply in the harness, drained from the massive rush of energy.

Ramone pulled her arm out slowly and then, her fist raised high, shiny with grease and pussyjuice, she walked triumphantly around the dance floor, showing off her arm like a treasure. The crowd cheered. A moment later, she slowly extracted the buttplug, glossy and pale pink. The crowd roared its approval at the sight of this device as well.

Seconds later, the audience's attention was diverted. A Mistress had sent her submissive to the bar to fetch a drink. As she had been commanded to do, the submissive returned to the dominatrix by walking in front of the women who were standing at the very edge of the dance floor, watching Marya and Ramone intently. They were furious at the slave for stepping in front of them, which was exactly the reaction the dominatrix had hoped for. Several of them lashed out at the poor, half-naked slave in their fury, and the woman tried her hardest to avoid spilling the drink.

She passed by Slash. Her Mistress brought her into Rough Trade regularly, and the slave both knew and feared Slash. As she passed, she murmured, "Please, pardon me, Mistress." She took two more steps and then—inexplicably—she fell.

She came down hard on the wooden floor, knocking the breath out of herself, sending herself sprawling. The drink spilled on several women nearby. The glass shattered on the floor. There was almost complete silence in the bar as the audience looked at her. The only sound was her tearful, desperate begging to her owner, now standing to look at her. "Please, Mistress, please forgive me! I did not mean to fall, I tripped accidentally. Please, Mistress, please forgive me!"

Slash smiled at the dominatrix, a friend she had known for many years. It was a smile that brought pleasure to the other dominatrixes in the room and chilled the blood of their submissives. "Laura, I'm afraid your slave has developed a bad case of the dropsy," she said. She indicated the harness that Marya had just left. "If you like, I invite you to make use of our facilities to improve her serving abilities."

To the delight of every woman in the room, dominant or otherwise, Laura smiled back at her friend. "Slash," she said, "you are most kind. I would be honored."

She nodded her approval to Ramone, who was wiping the grease from her arm, eager to be part of this interesting new diversion. The Japanese woman, her leather chaps snaking around her legs as she moved, walked toward the slave.

The woman was half-naked; her Mistress had permitted her a pair of loose white pants that contrasted with her chocolate skin, but her firm breasts were uncovered. Ramone grabbed her upper arm and pulled her toward the empty harness. It had been an object of pleasure when Marya used it; now it swung, a device of unspeakable horror.

The slave resisted. Ramone pulled on her, but the thin black woman tried to break away. Cherry came to assist, grabbing the woman's other arm, helping Ramone to drag her toward the center of the stage, under that hot white light.

Laura's piercing voice brought an immediate end to it. "Beth," she said, "you are worthless scum, a slave. I will not be embarrassed by the likes of you. You will do as you are told, or you will wish you had never been born."

The change was instantaneous. Beth stopped struggling immediately; she dropped her hands and stood, completely still, her head down. She did not want to be put into that harness; she already knew, as did everyone else in the room, what the punishment would be once she was strapped into it. But no matter what would happen in that harness, she would not disobey her Mistress's command. She would not embarrass her Mistress, not disregard an order for anything. She was submissive, her Mistress was dominant, and that was the end of that.

Laura and Slash moved into the bright circle of light

as Ramone and Cherry stripped and hoisted the slave, unwilling in spirit but reluctantly cooperative in body, into the harness. Laura, a stunningly beautiful, tall black woman sheathed in a form-fitting leather catsuit, tightened the buckles on the arm and leg loops. Marya, a willing participant, had rested her legs comfortably in the wide, loose leather straps. Beth had them buckled about her wrists and thighs so tightly that her flesh bulged out on either side of the leather restraints.

As her Mistress started to walk away, Beth decided to risk one final, all-out appeal for mercy. "Mistress!" she sobbed, as tears rolled down her cheeks. "Mistress, I beg of you, not in front of all these people! Mistress, I will do anything, anything, but please do not do this to me!"

Laura's voice was icy. "Another word and this will be the least of your troubles." Beth fell silent instantly, but as she turned away, Laura said to Ramone, "Is there anything we can do to guard against this happening again?"

Ramone smiled just as frostily as this Mistress. "I have just the thing," she said.

She bent down. The buttplug she had used on Marya was on the floor and she picked it up. She walked over to Beth, whose eyes had gone saucer-wide; she grabbed the back of Beth's head, put the rounded end of the buttplug against her lips, and pushed it hard into her mouth.

Beth choked and gagged. She tried to spit it out, but Ramone held it firmly. A scarf was produced from somewhere in the crowd. Ramone wrapped it around Beth's jaw, knotting it firmly at the back of her head to keep the plug in place. It was a giant pacifier, and Beth swallowed hard several times to control the nausea that rose in her stomach. She sagged in the harness, dejected; she knew that from this point on, it would only get worse.

From out of the crowd, a dominatrix held up a brown leather riding crop. Thanking this sexual sister, Laura took it and held it up to the crowd. She then offered it to Slash, as thanks for making her slave the subject of the evening's ridicule.

Slash took it and whacked it into her palm, making sure that Beth saw her and heard the crack of leather against skin. Then she walked around to the submissive's back. The strap that held her in against the harness was high up, just under her shoulder blades; most of her back and her buttocks were bare, begging for punishment.

"You embarrassed your Mistress; you spilled drinks on my patrons; you spoiled my glass," Slash told her. "I believe it is time to let you know that this is unacceptable."

Slash gave it to her. The first lash cut right across Beth's kidneys. The skin whitened across the stripe, then rose up in a cruel welt. The crowd roared; Slash felt like a gladiator in a Roman amphitheater, taking her strength from the audience's cruelty and desire to see this slave punished.

A second blow cracked against both of the slave's buttocks. Beth tried to scream, but the buttplug was tied firmly between her lips and her voice came out as a barely audible whine. Two more stripes were cracked across her kidneys, just to warm Slash up.

Now Slash hit her stride. Her breasts shook above their wire supports as her arm moved again and again, cracking the riding crop hard against Beth's back. The thin leather strap between her legs slipped sideways, exposing her slit, which was thick and hot with cuntjuice. She gave a dozen lashes, until Beth's back was crisscrossed with welts, and the slave had dissolved into tears and throat-rasping sobs.

Slash walked in front of the slave and thrust the tip of the crop, with its cruel leather tab, in her face. "When that plug is out of your mouth," Slash said, "you will kiss this crop and thank it for the punishment it has given you." Beth was unable to speak, but she nodded, her face shiny with tears.

Now Ramone and Laura came forward. Ramone once again picked up the jar of grease, but the amount she took was much smaller, just enough to lubricate her arm lightly. This time was not supposed to be easy. Laura, the arm of the leather suit pulled up, did the same. They then positioned themselves under their captive, ignoring her wide-eyed look of horror, her head shaking, begging them silently not to continue.

This time Laura took Beth's vagina. As Ramone had done with Marya, she made a fist and put her knuckles to the opening of Beth's ruby-red hole. But there was none of the slowness that Ramone had lavished on her friend. Instead, in a single, smooth, quick movement, the leather-suited dominatrix thrust her whole fist and half of her arm deep into Beth's cunt.

Beth screamed through the buttplug and closed her eyes, trying hard not to faint. Her cunt felt as if it had been pulled apart. It burned and ached from the rapid distending. After Beth thrust up and down a few times, however, and Beth became used to having a fist stuffed into her cunt, it became more bearable and even pleasurable. Never had she been touched by her Mistress before on her slit; her horror and agony were buffered by a feeling of wonder.

Ramone, who knew this would happen, had been watching closely. She watched the captive submissive's eyes, the expression in them, the tension in her body. Her own pussy throbbed when Laura's fist had first thrust home and Beth had bolted upright in pain. Now she watched the signals that Beth's body put out involuntarily for her to read. She waited for just that moment when the fisting ceased to be a punishment and started to become pleasant.

She moved so swiftly that few saw her begin, until they realized that her fist was just as deeply into Beth's asshole as Laura's arm was into her cunt.

For a couple of seconds, Beth fainted with the agony. Her head lolled to the side as she slipped into a merciful blackness. But another thrust, putting Ramone's whole arm into her rectum, brought her back to unrelenting reality. She longed to faint again but could not. Instead, she could only hang there, sobbing with agony, trying to pretend that it was just a nightmare.

Ramone grinned at Laura. She could feel the dominatrix's fist deep within the slave, feel the knuckles clearly through the perineum, the thin wall that separated rectum and pussytunnel. She wished she could grab Laura's hand with the slave's flesh in between, wrap her fingers around it, hold this dominatrix tight right through the very being of the slave.

To the delight of the audience and the misery of their prisoner, they made a game of it. They thrust up and down at the same time, fucking her in unison. Their fists pressed hard against each other as they slipped up and down the fleshy wall. Then they alternated; as Laura pushed in as far as she could, Ramone pulled out, until her knuckles were barely holding Beth's sphincter open. Then, as Laura pulled out her arm, slippery with grease and with the hot pussy juice that Beth was powerless to control, Ramone thrust her fist hard up into the depths of Beth's forbidden rear entrance.

The cuntjuice surprised Ramone, but Laura had

expected it. This was a slave who loved humiliation. She had been chained naked outside, forced to pleasure other slaves while dominatrixes looked on. She even reveled in being pissed upon. This punishment was horribly painful, but Laura knew that her little possession was, at the same time, turned on by the fact that she was being fist-fucked both ways in front of an entire room of women.

Of course, doing it to her was a turn-on for the nasty dominatrix, who could feel the leather catsuit becoming slippery between her thighs. Indeed, it was the best of both worlds for the pair.

The two leather-clad women nodded once to each other and then, together, as a single unit, thrust upward. Both of their arms disappeared almost to their elbows, and Beth screamed so loudly that women in the back of the bar could hear her clearly, right through her buttplug gag.

Then they pulled out completely, and Beth groaned loudly and hung limply in the harness. While she no longer had the agony of both of her cavities split open as wide as they would go, both of them burned, horribly raw, with the invasion. She did not believe she had ever been hurt so badly. But at the same time, in the mysterious way of bondage, she looked over at her triumphant Mistress and felt her heart swell with pride. Her Mistress was exuberant, excited, triumphant. The knowledge that she had caused this made the pain not only bearable, but pleasurable. Beth knew that it would be days before she would be back to normal. Until then, every step, every agonizing movement, would bring back this wonderful moment vividly to her.

The two women on the floor raised their fists to the audience, basking in the applause and cheers. Ramone's hand was stained with thin, watery blood; Laura's had pussyjuice mixed with the caramel-colored grease, all the proof the Mistresses in the bar needed to see, to confirm their knowledge that these worthless slaves were so lowly they couldn't even differentiate between pleasure and pain. The submissives in the crowd shivered, bone-chilled, hoping against hope that their dominatrixes would not want to act out a similar scene on them.

"You can leave her hanging there for the rest of the night, if you desire," Slash said to Laura, who had taken the towel offered to her and was wiping the grease and fluid from her arm.

"Thank you, I think I will," Laura said. "Slash, that was absolutely wonderful. Why you don't have a stable of your own slaves is beyond me. When it comes to punishing a submissive, I have never seen such a resourceful woman."

"Running this bar takes all my time," Slash replied. "Besides, this way I can punish slaves any time I want, right here on the middle of the floor, and have women lining up outside the door to see it."

With the familiarity of long friendship, Laura reached up to kiss her friend full on the lips. "Well, you punished mine very well tonight. In fact, I think I just might have to get one of those harnesses for myself."

She turned to another Mistress, who wanted to ask some questions, and Slash walked back to Ramone, who was wiping off her arm and marveling at how many women were now clustered around the hanging submissive, examining the leather harness and the way it held its prey so effectively.

"You should have bought shares in the company that sells those devices," Ramone laughed. "Judging by how many women are saying they're going to buy one tomorrow, we'd be millionaires."

"You're probably right," Slash said as she watched them. She then bent down, wetting a finger, to wipe a black mark off the side of one impeccably shiny leather boot.

Her action caught Ramone's eye; Slash would never have come downstairs with a mark on her boot. Strangely enough, the mark was the same color as the shoes that the submissive Beth had been wearing when she had walked back from the bar with her Mistress's drink, balanced so carefully, before she fell.

"Slash!" Ramone couldn't help grinning wildly. "Now, how on earth did that happen? You—no, not you—you wouldn't have maybe stepped forward at the wrong time, would you?"

"Depends." Slash tried her best not to grin, too. "The wrong time—or maybe the right time."

Ramone took her friend by the waist and accepted a kiss. "I always said that you had impeccable timing," she exclaimed.

Chapter Ten

Slash put away the last glass, swiped the rag once more over the spotless bar, and then sighed most uncharacteristically.

She was bummed out, and she was furious at herself for being that way. She put away the containers of cut fruit for the drinks, slamming the lids down much harder than necessary. She had no right to be bummed, she told herself, and yet…she was.

It was Slash's birthday. She was unhappy because the night had gone on like every other night—providing she could call two dykes eating each other to climax on the dance floor, two doing exactly the same thing on the table at a booth, and Cherry taking a virgin right in the open an average night. She was bummed because no one had even acknowledged her birthday, much less done anything about it.

She was furious at herself because she had always kept the date a secret. There was no fuss about it because no one knew. She kept it a secret because she didn't want anyone to fuss about her, and yet here she was, alone in the bar, moping about because—even she couldn't figure this one out—no one had made the fuss she didn't want. She was furious because she knew she shouldn't have expected anything, furious because she was upset about something that didn't matter. Fuck, she was upset with herself just because she never got upset about anything! And that just made it all worse, because if she'd been asked, Slash couldn't possibly have explained why she even cared about something as mundane as a birthday. Tits were special, cunts were special, dykes held close to her in the middle of the night were special—but birthdays? She hated the side of her brain that was making such an issue out of it.

She started to get everything ready for the next evening, to avoid having to do it later, but her heart wasn't in it. "Fuck it!" She slammed the cash register shut angrily. "It can wait." The waitresses had all gone home, and even Ramone, who usually closed up with her, had begged off early. For a long time she debated going down the street to a nearby restaurant to celebrate with her favorite treat, a glass of champagne and an ice-cold platter of raw oysters, but the thought of sitting by herself at such a feast seemed too depressing. "Fuck it again!" she said. "I might as well go to bed."

She turned out the last bank of lights and, almost wearily, climbed the staircase to her loft. Her private residence was dark, which surprised her; she thought she had left the light on in the bedroom. She flicked the switch, and the room was flooded with light.

"Surprise!"

For one moment, Slash was taken aback. Then, as her eyes adjusted to the sudden light, a broad grin grew across her face. There were helium balloons and streamers hanging in the air. A huge banner across one wall read "Happy Birthday Slash." Standing in front of all this, equally huge grins across their faces and ridiculous pointed party hats on their heads, were Cherry, Stef, and Ramone.

"What's this—how—how did you know?" Slash said. She kept looking at the balloons and the streamers with an almost-childlike joy that her three friends had never before seen in their lives.

Ramone laughed. "Do you remember that time you had to renew your insurance, and you were so busy you asked me to do it?" Slash nodded. "Well, I had to have your birthdate, right? So I just kept that information in case it might come in handy sometime."

Stef laughed, too. "Slash, you really surprised me," she said. "You've been miserable all day because no one did anything. Oh, you shake your head, but I know better! You're tough and cool, but you're human too!"

Slash looked around again and then laughed, a very rare sound from this haughty woman. "Okay, you got me. I guess I was kind of depressed about it. But now this…you guys are great. It's really fabulous to have friends like you. How did you get all this done up here?"

"I figured if we all left early, you'd stay in the bar and do the closing up by yourself," Ramone said. "I'm sorry I left all the work downstairs to you. But we had to make sure that you didn't come up before we were ready."

Just then the telephone rang; Slash went for it, but Ramone put up a hand to stop her before she could pick it up first. Slash heard her giving directions to the little-known outside entrance to the upstairs loft.

"Your present's on its way over," Ramone said. Slash protested that she didn't need a present, but Ramone said, "Of course you do!—it's your birthday. And we happen to know that it's exactly what you want. In the meantime, though, can we interest you in a little preliminary gift while we're waiting?"

The three of them moved toward Slash. She put her hands up to touch them, but Stef put them back at her side gently. "It's your birthday," she said. "This is when we do the work, and you do nothing but sit back, relax, and enjoy it."

Slash did. As the trio undressed her, they undressed themselves slowly. The buttons of Slash's shirt were opened in leisurely fashion, with Stef licking her throat and chest as more and more was revealed, finally working to her tits once they were freed from the cloth. Cherry was on her knees, opening the buttons on Slash's fly, and putting her tongue into the opening to kiss the rich brown skin under it. Ramone was at Slash's mouth, and the two pushed their tongues into each other, moaning and sighing softly as they did.

When all of them were naked, they led Slash into the bedroom. The bed was also decorated with balloons and streamers, and Slash murmured happily as they laid her on the spotless comforter and climbed on the bed with her.

Cherry moved up to her head; Slash was allowed to expend the tiny effort to touch the gold ring that went through her nipple, a ring that had always fascinated and excited her, although when she tried to reach for Cherry's other breast she was told she was supposed to relax and let them make love to her. Cherry bent over her and their mouths met, first in a light kiss and shortly afterwards in deep, lingering, hungry kisses that at once satisfied them and left them wanting more.

Stef went to Slash's tits. She loved to touch them—"chocolate kisses," she called them—and to take them into her mouth and watch her saliva turn the deep brown skin rich and shiny. She drew each one in and used her tongue and teeth to tease the nipple into standing up hard and straight out from the warm firmness of Slash's breast. A quick bite, a long lap, and Slash groaned. It felt as if there were nerves that ran directly from her tits to her crotch, and every movement of Stef's mouth on her nipple sent electric impulses through those nerves that pooled at her pussy and sent the huge nubbin of her clit throbbing with need.

Ramone was waiting at that crotch. She watched it, fascinated, pulling the swollen lips apart to have a better look. She could actually see Slash's crotch turn juicy. The liquid seeped out of her hole, making the entrance shiny, spreading to the rest of her slit. It was also possible to see the clit grow in size, becoming hard and engorging with blood and sexual tension. Ramone loved watching Slash become turned on. When she bent down and applied the tip of her tongue, Slash's hips rose off the bed instantly, to push her clit against the heat of Ramone's expert pussy-eating mouth.

Ramone folded her tongue against her lips to form a scoop, and she used this to lap the entire length of Slash's cunt, from bottom to top. The pussyjuice collected in the fold, and she ran her tongue over the roof of her mouth to savor its hot richness. She stayed like that for a long time, until the very last bit of flavor was gone. Then she was right back at Slash's cunt, sliding up and down on it so intensely that she simply held out her tongue and moved her head.

The otherwise-empty loft was noisy with the sounds of their moans, of kisses and tongues lapping. The perfume of hot pussy hung in the air as thick as smoke. Slash couldn't imagine any birthday present that could possibly compare with this.

Slash wasn't the only one who was receiving pleasure from this. Cherry stayed with her, kissing her long and hard, then stopping to move down her neck, to run a tongue in the folds of her ear and kiss at her throat. Stef was making love to Slash's tits, but at the same time, her body was turned so that her own naked cunt was close to Cherry. With a free hand, Cherry was fingering Stef's pussy; her other hand was busy between the cuntlips of her own.

Slash was just lying there, drinking in all of the attention. For as strong a woman as she was, it was still almost indescribably pleasant to lose control to these trusted friends. She floated along the wave of delightful sensations that coursed through her body from her face, her tits, her cunt, and the attention being paid to each.

Ramone used the end of her tongue to burrow into Slash's cunt. The shape fitted as perfectly into the triangle at the top of the slit as jigsaw-puzzle pieces do. With her tongue entrenched firmly, she moved it back and forth, taking the clit with it. Slash loved this and moaned loudly as Ramone hastened her movements. Her lips and chin were soaked with cuntjuice; her mouth was filled with it. Her fingers were exploring Slash's slit even as her tongue did; one fingertip teased the slope at the opening of Slash's vagina, another fingertip danced lightly over her asshole, dipping less than a hairbreadth inside, just enough to stretch the muscles and expose the velvety membrane that lined the forbidden avenue.

It was enough to send Slash over the edge. She lifted her hips off the bed, bucking them against Ramone's tongue, a movement that the Japanese woman knew as intimately as her own. She stepped up her licking on the rockhard button and then rode it out as Slash came, trembling, moaning, shaking.

They had all been so involved that they never heard the knocking at the door until it became an incessant pounding. "I forgot about her!" Ramone shrieked, as she jumped off the bed and hurried to the door. "Boy, is she going to be pissed off!"

She might have been, but when the woman at the door looked at Ramone, naked, her hair mussed, her lips and chin shiny with pussyjuice, her annoyed expression immediately changed to one of understanding and approval. "What a shame I was on the other side of the door," she said as she stepped inside. "It looks like I'm missing a pretty fantastic party."

The visitor, whose name was Jayne, was introduced to Slash and Stef; she already knew Cherry, whom she greeted with a hug and kiss. She did not seem the least bit surprised to be invited into a room where four women were enjoying each other, so Stef and Slash were not the least bit concerned about being introduced to this woman while they were naked, Slash obviously relaxing from a massive orgasm. Jayne was a beautiful woman with amazingly thick brown hair and full, sensual lips; she wore a well-tailored suit and carried an old-fashioned doctor's bag, crafted in heavy black leather, which she set down on the floor. She looked like a Wall Street businesswoman, save for one peculiarity: each of her ears had been pierced four times through the fleshy lobes and were adorned with gold rings in descending sizes. On her right ear, a thin gold chain ran through the four rings, binding them to each other. The end of the chain hung halfway down to Jayne's shoulder, ending in an enameled pink triangle.

Slash, who was open to any scenario her friends might come up with, was still curious. She vaguely remembered Jayne's face; she believed she had seen her before in the bar, although the beautiful woman had never done anything out of the ordinary while she was there. Who was this woman, and why was she here? Slash could pick up a casual lover at any time, of any persuasion, simply by walking through her own bar, so it had to be more than that. There had to be a special wrinkle to all of this. Slash could hardly wait to find out what it was.

Ramone knew this, so she dragged it out as long as possible, teasing her friend. "We all got together to give you a present, Slash," she said. "We've always considered ourselves to be one family, and since this is the first time we've celebrated your birthday, we wanted it to be something you'd remember and treasure for a long time."

"We thought about things you've talked about in the past," Cherry said. "What's the one thing you've always said you wanted to do, if you could only get a few minutes away from the bar to do it?"

Slash turned to them in mock surprise, her eyes wide. "You mean Jayne is going to take me on that cruise around the world?" she asked.

Everyone laughed, and Ramone teased, "We'd go for that only if we could all go with you, and you know how much our boss pays us." She smiled. "Maybe we'll work on that for another year. No, what is it you're always talking about?"

Slash was mystified. "I don't know, I really don't

remember talking about anything." She looked around at all of them, and then noticed that Cherry was playing with the gold ring in her nipple slowly and pointedly. "That's it!" the black woman said. "I've always said I'd get a nipple ring like Cherry's, except I'm always too busy."

"Exactly!" Ramone gestured to Jayne. "You couldn't leave the bar to get to the piercing studio, so we brought the piercer to you."

Once again, Slash's love and admiration for these closest friends welled up. "That's so good of all of you," she said. "You're right—I certainly will treasure it. I can't believe you remembered me talking about that and then set up all of this. It's wonderful!"

Ramone had cleared off the bedside table. Jayne put up her medical bag, opened the heavy clasp, and set out her instruments. Slash was fascinated. "Jayne did my nipple ring and the ones in my pussy," Cherry said, and Jayne nodded as she laid out the forceps, the needle, the sterilizing baths. "She did all of Kiki's piercings, too. She's one of the best."

"Which one do you want done?" Jayne asked.

Slash thought about it for a long time. "If it doesn't overstep what they've paid you...could you do them both?"

Jayne looked at Cherry. They both laughed. "Cherry told me almost word for word what you'd say," the brunette said. "That's why I brought along two rings, just in case."

She looked at Slash's tits carefully, but even though she had an almost-clinical detachment on the outside, the women could clearly see by her expression and her light touch that she was thrilled to be close to such a body. There was just cause for that; lying on the white comforter, her magnificent body stretched out full, her flawless skin a chocolate hue under the lights, her tits straight up with hard nipples, her pussy still wet from her recent orgasm, Slash had to be every woman's dream.

"They're going to be sore and tender for a while," Jayne told her. "It takes time for the wounds to heal."

"Then we'd better give them something to remember," Ramone said. "Can you wait just a bit, Jayne?"

"Only if I get to help," Jayne replied.

Cherry grinned at her; she had wondered secretly how long her friend would be able to sit there so prim and proper in her tailored suit, surrounded by four naked, lusty women. When Jayne took off her jacket and started to unbutton her shirt, Cherry's smile became that of a co-conspirator; she was waiting to see the looks on her friends' faces.

Jayne obviously believed in her craft. In addition to the eight rings in her ears, she displayed her full, firm tits, each with a gold ring through the nipple. When she unbuttoned the waistband of her skirt she revealed a ring embedded in the flesh of her navel. But there was even more to come.

She dropped the skirt to the floor; she was wearing nothing under it. She sank into the chair by the bed, leaned back, and spread her legs to give them all a chance to look.

Like Cherry, she had gold rings set into her pussylips, one on either side of her vagina. These were further adorned. A length of fine gold chain, the thinnest possible, was attached to each ring. They met over the entrance to her hole, brought together and held by a tiny gold padlock.

The women were transfixed. They got off the bed and came over to see, intrigued by this most unusual body jewelry.

The padlock was the size of a penny, thin and wrought magnificently. It was heart-shaped, decorated on the back with a single tiny diamond chip. On the front was the lock; now they noticed that Jayne also wore a gold necklace, with a tiny key for the pendant.

"Are there other keys?" Ramone asked.

Jayne said, "There is one other, and one day another woman may wear it around her neck. Until then, both keys remain in my keeping. I open this lock according to my own needs and desires."

So saying, she reached behind her neck and opened the chain, handing it to Cherry, who inserted the delicate key into the lock and turned it. The miniature mechanism opened, and Jayne took the padlock off the chains. They hung invitingly from each cunt-ring.

"First, though, I think we should get down to business," the piercer said. They went back to the bed, where once again Slash became the center of attention.

It was time for each of them to wish a temporary farewell to her nipples. In turn, each woman took the swollen nubs into her mouth, sucking with her lips, teasing with her tongue, kissing them as she moved away. Jayne watched them longingly; when all had finished, Slash motioned to her as well. The new member of their circle came over and took Slash's nipples into her mouth hungrily. Slash was pleased when Jayne ran her hands slowly over the perfect black skin; indicating that they would not finish this birthday party without the full participation of this woman.

But once she had kissed Slash's tits, Jayne was back to business, a professional about to render the service she had been paid to perform. The fact that she was doing it while she was completely naked, all of her gold rings gleaming in the lights that had been turned up for her to work, made her no less so, and only added to her allure.

Using an alcohol swab, she cleaned Slash's right nipple and the area around it thoroughly. The dark skin shone in the light as if it had been waxed.

"This might hurt a bit," Jayne warned her patient, as the other three women looked on in fascination.

Slash didn't mind at all. "I've been looking forward to this for so long, it's going to be a pleasure," she replied.

Jayne used forceps with loops at the end, which she closed firmly around Slash's nipple. Holding it firmly with one hand, she picked up the long, thick needle with the other. Ramone found herself holding her breath along with Slash as the razor-sharp point of the needle was held at the forceps loop, pricking against Slash's nipple.

"Are you ready?" Jayne asked. Slash nodded.

The needle went into the flesh like it was butter. In Jayne's experienced hands, it passed through the forceps, through the nipple, and came out the other side. Jayne took it from there, pulling it through the flesh. Slash let out her breath slowly as the needle passed through her body and finally exited, leaving the perfectly round hole behind.

Jayne worked smoothly and quickly, putting down the forceps and opening the gold ring. She slipped it into the hole, closed it, and then took her fingers away; the ring was a perfect gold sphere nesting in the thick, dimpled flesh.

Slash looked down with satisfaction. The gold was set off beautifully by her dark skin. She held her breast up to see it—gingerly, for the nipple was tender. "Do you want the second one done now?" Jayne asked.

"Of course," Slash said. "I want a matching set."

Once again the forceps closed around a nipple, the needle was inserted, and then drawn firmly through the flesh to open a hole that was immediately filled with the precious metal. When it was done, Ramone bent down and kissed all around the rings, on the firm skin of Slash's tits, and longed for the moment when the piercings would be healed enough to allow her to take the nipples themselves into her mouth and run her lips around the gold rings, poke the end of her tongue through them, suck them into her mouth, hold them with her teeth.

"You are very good at that," Slash said as Jayne cleaned up her instruments and put everything back into the black leather doctor's bag. "I never realized it went so quickly and smoothly, and I hardly felt anything other than excitement."

"I'll be the first to admit that this was one of the easiest I have ever done," Jayne said. "There's something about working without the restrictions of clothing that seems to make it go better."

Slash said, "Since we're both naked, can I thank you for the job you've done?"

Jayne nodded enthusiastically. "Then you won't be the only one here fulfilling a fantasy," she admitted. "I've always thought you were one of the most exciting women I've ever seen. From the very first time I saw you, I've dreamed about making love to you."

Slash motioned for her to come over. "There's no use having a fantasy if you can't fulfill it."

At Slash's direction, Jayne came over to where the lanky black woman was stretched on the bed. Now that the actual piercing was done, Ramone lowered the bright lights, and Jayne took a moment to admire Slash in the subdued atmosphere. The gold rings gleamed against the darkness of her body and as she spread her thighs, Jayne could see the traces of wetness on her pussylips.

Jayne positioned herself above Slash, as the three friends looked on. Slash took the delightfully fleshy buttocks in her hands and pulled Jayne's cunt over her face. On her hands and knees, her face over Slash's wet pussy, Jayne looked at the tight, curly hair; the swollen lips; and the strong thighs for just a moment before she buried herself deep in Slash's crotch. Once she felt the hot tongue on her own clit, Slash pulled Jayne down to her and licked at a pussy that was equally swollen and wet.

The others spurred them on. As Jayne and Slash sixty-nined, their tongues working deep in each other's soaked slits, Cherry came over and caressed their bodies. She ran her hands all over Jayne's back and then grabbed her buttocks, above Slash's hands.

She knew Jayne intimately, knew what she liked. She wetted a finger, and while Slash concentrated with her mouth on Jayne's clit, Cherry put her fingertip at the opening to Jayne's anus. As smoothly as the needle that had gone through Slash's nipple, Cherry's finger opened the tight ring of muscles and gained access to the fiery tunnel. Jayne groaned loudly and increased her efforts on Slash's cunt.

Ramone and Stef were not to be left out, but for the moment, they let the three on the bed alone. Slash had a thick, soft rug beside her bed and the two of them were on this, stretched out on the floor. They were lying opposite each other, their legs scissored over, their pussies firmly touching together. By bucking their hips up and down and lifting their asses off the floor, they were able to rub their cunts together, and their excited groans of delight matched those of the women licking and sucking on the bed beside them.

Ramone and Stef came first, the Japanese woman crying out her pleasure as she rubbed furiously on Stef's cunt; when she was finished, she turned around and used the fingers of both hands to bring Stef off. Stef actually came twice, the first a shiver that both satisfied and left her wanting more at the same time. Moments later, the second climax was a tidal wave that swept right through her and left her quivering and moaning on the floor.

Jayne, her tongue on a hot clit, Slash's own mouth on her own, was further excited by Cherry, who was fucking her ass with a finger. Now Slash, feeling her own passions start to rise in the unmistakable way of climax, concentrated on Jayne's clit. She was fucking it, making love to it, sucking it hard, and Jayne responded. She was a screamer, and the loft echoed with the sounds of her joyous cries.

She didn't cry out for long, though, because she wanted to give back to Slash what Slash had given to her. Seconds later, her head was back between the ebony thighs. She licked harder and faster than she thought she ever could. Finally, Slash let herself go, dissolving into the depths of the orgasm that took over her entire body.

Later, there was a cake; the three women had thought of everything. Cherry turned out the lights as Ramone came into the bedroom, illuminated by the candles on the baked treat. Slash, who ordinarily shunned sweets, surprised everyone by eating two slices.

"I have to," she explained. "It isn't every day that I get my first birthday cake."

"Your *first* one?" Stef asked in surprise. "Come on,

Slash, didn't you have birthday parties when you were a kid?"

Slash smiled. "Sounds like something a psychiatrist would have a field day with, doesn't it? Well, I didn't turn out to be a mass murderer or anything just because I never got a birthday cake. But it did teach me to be especially grateful when the best friends a woman could ever have get together and throw me a party. How did you know chocolate was my favorite flavor, anyway?"

It was Ramone's turn to laugh. "You thought we ignored you when you mentioned the nipple ring, too."

Slash looked down and touched them, gently, for they were still very sore. "You were right about that one," she said. "It's a present I'll never forget. How can I? Every time I take off my shirt, I'm going to be turned on by my own tits."

Cherry replied, "If you aren't turned on by those tits, you'll be the only woman in New York City who isn't. Now, did anyone bring a pin-the-tail-on-the-donkey game? After all, this is supposed to be a birthday party!"

Chapter Eleven

"Oh, Slash," the blonde woman said, as she took her drink, "that is just so utterly amazing. It is just so ace!"

Slash barely acknowledged her, with a straight-faced expression, nodding slightly as she reached for a glass to fill another order.

Despite Slash's lack of interest, the woman continued to babble. "I've always been turned on by something like that," she went on. "Oh, I could make you happy, Slash. I've got something special. What do you say, Slash? Later, maybe?"

Slash scowled at her. "Don't sit up for me," she said.

The woman was oblivious to the insult. "I'll be waiting." She put her fingers to her mouth and blew Slash a kiss before she walked away from the bar and melted into the crowd.

"Who the fuck was that?" Slash asked.

Ramone laughed. "I don't know, but you sure made an impression on her. Of course, it's pretty easy to see why. I think you've made an impression on everyone here tonight—me included."

Slash looked down at herself and, modesty aside, she had to agree with her friend's assessment. In honor of the evening's entertainment, which was proving so popular that the lineup outside the door went around the block, she had chosen a particularly striking costume.

She wore nothing above her waist except for a large gold ring through one earlobe, and her birthday present, the two gold rings through her nipples. The piercings had healed almost completely. To further adorn them on this, the first night she had exposed them in the bar, she had snapped a thin gold chain onto the rings. The chain hung between them, joining them with a gold line across her chest. Every woman in the bar wanted to hold that chain between her fingers and tug on the rings.

She wore a pair of brilliant red satin boxer shorts with a wide white elastic waistband. Her feet were laced into high black wrestling boots with heavy soles and long white laces. As a finishing touch, she had oiled every inch of her skin, which shone under the lights and accentuated every ripple of her muscular body. She couldn't go anywhere in the bar without lusting eyes following her every move. Seldom had she ever looked better than she did this night.

A submissive came up to the bar, moving in at the corner, trying to get close enough to order without annoying any of the women already there; one might be a Mistress, who might not like the idea of a slave trying to get past her. Slash saw her and winked at Ramone; Slash was in a particularly cruel mood this evening. She hadn't baited a submissive in a long time.

She left the submissive cooling her heels for a while, enjoying the woman's pained expression; it was obvious that she had been sent to fetch a drink for her Mistress, who must not be kept waiting. Slash kept her just long enough to ensure that she would be disciplined for taking so long, without leaving her so long that the Mistress would become angry with Slash for ignoring a paying customer. Slash knew exactly when the line was crossed, and she kept to schedule with just a few moments to spare.

"A Scotch, please, Mistress," the submissive said, keeping her eyes lowered. She had been coming to Rough Trade for several years and knew that while Slash was not primarily a dominatrix, she never turned down an opportunity to participate in a good B&D scene, which was why she used the proper term of respect when ordering. To a submissive, any dominatrix was a Mistress and must always be addressed as such.

Slash knew the submissive's Mistress well and reached for her favorite brand, adding only as much ice as she knew the woman preferred. Slash took the money offered, counting out the change exactly, and while the submissive dared not count it in front of the bartender— implying that she mistrusted her—she looked at it quickly and took out the coins she had been commanded to leave as a tip. She sighed with relief when she realized that Slash had not played one of her favorite tricks. Since she knew precisely how generous her regular customers were, Slash often made change in such a way that it was difficult or impossible to come up with the exact amount the submissive had been ordered to leave from the coins that Slash handed back. She loved to watch the submissives, tongue-tied with nervousness, try to ask Slash to exchange the coins for denominations they could leave for the correct tip.

She decided to have her fun in a different way. Just before the young woman, who was dressed in a loose shift with a dog collar around her throat, picked up the glass to leave, Slash said, "You understand that you must obey every dominatrix, don't you?"

"Yes, Mistress." She was At Slash's words, cold ran right through the submissive. She knew she was being set up, but was powerless to do anything but play right into the bartender's hands.

"Including me?"

"Absolutely, Mistress." Her voice was so low that it was difficult to hear her over the noise of the crowd.

"Where is your Mistress sitting?" The submissive indicated a woman waiting alone at a table close to the bar, on Slash's left side. "Then," the half-naked bartender said, "you will go this way." She indicated the right side of the building. "You will go all around the room, by the walls, in front of the telephones. You will go over by the windows. You will make a big circle of the bar on your way back to your Mistress's table. Is this understood?"

"Yes, Mistress." The submissive's tongue felt swollen and woolly inside her mouth; it was difficult to get the words out. She would disobey another Mistress's command only if it directly contradicted an order given her by her owner. In this case, her Mistress had not indicated a specific route back to the table from the bar; so, preparing for the worst, the submissive took the long way.

Slash watched her go, making a circle of the bar. When she got to the table, Slash couldn't hear them, but she could see that the Mistress was displeased. The submissive blurted out an explanation, but it was too late for that; the Mistress stood up, knocked her slave to the floor with a single open-handed slap, and then picked up a riding crop that was on the table beside her. She stood over the slave, lying on the floor, and raised the crop again and again, bringing it down on the lowly submissive's body. Now Slash could hear the submissive's cries of pain and pleas for mercy over the noisy crowd. When the Mistress was finished, she turned in Slash's direction. Instead of being upset with the bartender, she raised the riding crop in triumph and nodded a thank-you for giving her a reason to punish her slave.

Her mean streak appeased for a while, Slash turned to Ramone and said, "Can you watch the bar for a few minutes? I want to check on the ring."

"Bar is watched," Ramone replied and stared in open admiration as Slash walked past her, satin boxers and oiled skin gleaming in the colored lights.

All eyes on her, the crowd parted to let her through. "Love your tit rings, Slash!" one yelled out. Another woman purred, "Slash, honey, I'd give the moon to swing on your chain."

Slash acknowledged them all. "Hang tight, ladies. Once our entertainment gets going, I'm going to be so hot, I'm going to need someone to suck my pussy."

The bar was especially packed this evening because most of the dance floor was gone. Slash walked over to it. A bank of hot white lights lit it up, providing a focal point that already had women so excited that several of them were being eaten even as they sat at their tables, with their lovers on the floor between their legs.

The hardwood dance floor was covered with a boxing ring. It was almost regulation size, built on a platform. It had been on the dance floor for three nights now, unused. Slash could have had it built in a single afternoon if she had wanted to, but instead she left it there, empty, forbidding anyone to enter it, simply to heighten everyone's interest. Her strategy had worked. The crowd was almost in a frenzy, waiting for the entertainment to begin this evening.

· Slash walked all around it. The canvas floor was new, unmarked. The ropes were thick and strong, padded around the upright posts, and Slash pulled on them, testing their resistance. They had good elasticity, but they would also hold someone in if necessary.

There was a bank of stairs leading up to it, but they had been roped off to prevent bar patrons from entering the ring. Slash longed to do so, but restrained herself. There would be plenty of time later on. She had to admit that she was just as eager for the show as the women in the bar.

"Hey, Slash!" a woman called from a table nearby. "Is this show going to be everything you said?"

Slash turned to her; under the hot lights, her oiled skin looked like onyx. "Have I ever delivered less than I've promised?"

"You've got me there," the woman admitted. "I guess that's why I'll keeping coming here until the building finally crumbles into dust."

Slash went back to the bar. "The show starts in another hour," she said to Ramone. "Have those sluts shown up yet?"

"One just came in the door." Ramone indicated a woman who was walking toward them. "The other just called; she's on her way."

"Send her in when she arrives," Slash said. "I'll be in the office in the back. I want to make sure they're dressed exactly the way I want them. After all, we have a show to put on.

At precisely the stroke of midnight, just as she had promised, Slash had Kiki turn up the hot white lights over the boxing ring. A cheer went up from the crowd, many of whom had been standing beside the ring since late afternoon to get a choice position.

Under the lights, Slash's oiled body was licorice, and the rings in her nipples gleamed fiercely. She went up the stairs and slipped between the ropes into the ring, where Cherry handed her a microphone.

"Ladies and...well, ladies and ladies!" she said, mocking a boxing announcer's booming overemphasis. "Tonight, as promised, we bring you the event you've all been waiting for. Live from Rough Trade, we present the bout of the century!"

The crowd cheered again, and Slash felt as if she was really in the middle of a boxing match, what with the smoke and the tension from the crowd. But this was entirely different; it was a match the patrons would never forget.

Cherry and Stef had been recruited to act as managers, for Slash would never put on a show that didn't have all the pomp of the real thing, and now these two women, dressed in colorful satin jackets, went to the back of the bar, to the rooms where the two fighters waited to be called.

"We couldn't decide whether to put on boxing or wrestling," Slash continued. "So we compromised; this will be a bit of both. Quite simply, there are no rules." A murmur of approval went around the room. "There are no rounds, no referee. It is over when one of the combatants decides it is finished, when she knows she cannot go on."

What she did not mention, but which had been the stuff of rumors ever since the match had been announced, was that the winner of the bout received not only her evening's pay, but a $10,000 bonus. Slash was determined to give the crowd their due, and she did not want a half-assed match with the women simply going through the motions. The large purse would make for an interesting evening.

"In this corner"—Slash indicated it with a wide sweep of her arm—"wearing yellow tonight, we present Lucy!"

A path had been cleared through the crowd, and Cherry, wearing her bright yellow satin jacket, walked ahead of a woman who was outfitted in a full-length satin robe. Both of them went up the stairs and climbed into the ring, where Slash indicated that Lucy should come to the center of the ring. When she did, Slash grabbed the robe by the collar and ripped it away.

The crowd gasped as one, and then burst into applause. Lucy was something they had never seen before at Rough Trade.

Slash had specifically ordered Lucy to look almost like a centerfold from a men's magazine, just for the shock value. Lucy had spent a lot of time on her appearance; her long blonde hair, so light it was almost white, was teased and coiffed carefully. She was tall and thin, with tits so large and firm they almost didn't look real. She was obviously a bodybuilder, but she wasn't overly muscular—just very lean and strong. Her legs were impossibly long, her hips wide, her stomach flat. To show all of this off, her yellow costume consisted of a string bikini that covered barely more than her huge nipples. The bikini bottom hooked up high over her hips, went down to a small triangle over her cunt, and ended in a thong that went up the crack of her ass between gorgeously proportioned asscheeks. She was a man's wet-dream girl. She was the woman millions of young men jacked off to between the pages of a magazine. She was so gorgeous she couldn't possibly be real—and yet here she was in the ring at Rough Trade. Best of all, she was a dyke!

"And in the other corner—may we present Karen!"

Stef, in a bright green jacket, led this fighter to the ring. Her hair was as artfully arranged as Lucy's, except that it was a rich brunette. She stepped into the ring as well, sizing up the almost-naked Lucy with narrow eyes; she wanted the prize money desperately. At a motion from Slash, she went to the center of the ring, where her green satin robe was held at the neck and pulled dramatically from her body.

She was as magnificent as Lucy; in fact, Slash had chosen them carefully so that they were almost evenly matched. Her tits were also huge, so firm and placed so high on her chest that they didn't seem real, and they were barely covered by her green bikini. Her stomach was washboard-flat, her mound firm and gently rounded, her cunt covered by a triangle of green fabric, her asscheeks divided by the green thong that went between them and met the waistband looping up over her hips.

Through the bright light, Slash could see money changing hands in the crowd, and she knew that small fortunes would be won and lost this evening. She already had a couple of small side bets going with women who knew the fighters, but her interest went much deeper than money. She wanted to see these women grapple; she wanted to see them fight.

She turned off the microphone and faced the women. "You know the story," she said. "No rules. We don't stop the fight, and there's no draw here—only a winner. That winner takes home ten grand over her wages. And there had better be a hell of show for these women, or no one gets the money, winner or not. Clear?" The women nodded.

"Then," Slash said as she gathered up the microphone cord and headed toward the ropes, "you're on your own."

As she stepped out of the ring, all attention turned from her to the show in the center of the floor. The two women, looking more like fashion models than fighters, were circling each other slowly, sizing each other up. Each was looking for the place she would attack first, trying to sense the other's weakness. They were like predators after their prey. Then Slash picked up the hammer and banged the bell.

Now they were in earnest, still circling warily. The crowd, all of whom were standing, was almost silent. The entire room was focused on the two; every woman in the room was waiting, holding her breath.

Lucy moved first. The blonde woman, her thick hair swinging, leaped forward. Karen was waiting for her, and they met in the center of the ring, their hands grasped around each other's forearms, trying to knock each other off balance. Like sumo wrestlers they pushed back and forth, each looking to gain the upper hand.

With a shout of anger, Karen tipped her body sideways. Lucy, all her weight forward, went with her and fell heavily to the mat. Karen was on top of her in a second, straddling her body. Only the small triangle of green fabric separated her cunt from Lucy's body—a cunt that, to her own surprise, was fiercely hot and wet. As much as she had geared her mind to fighting, to winning the prize, Karen was excited, and so was Lucy.

Karen raised her arm to strike, but Lucy caught her wrist. Their muscles trembled as they struggled, Karen to free herself and Lucy to push her opponent away. It seemed like an eternity before Lucy gave a mighty heave and pushed the brunette off her and to the mat. Before she could take the advantage, though, Karen was on her feet. Lucy jumped up as well. They faced each other again.

"Fight, dyke! Fight, dyke! Fight, dyke!" It was a chant the crowd took up. The women in the audience were thoroughly enjoying themselves. To see such perfect pinups disheveled, sweaty, panting—it was marvelous! Those luscious globular tits heaving, those perfect cunts covered with a scrap of fabric, those beautiful faces distorted with fury—Slash had outdone herself once again.

With a roar of anger Lucy flung herself at Karen. She caught her waist and drove her into the ropes, where, momentarily, Karen was unable to do anything. Lucy drove her fist twice into Karen's stomach, then grabbed a handful of the brunette's hair and used it to fling Karen heavily onto the mat. She threw herself at the prone fighter, but Karen rolled out of the way and Lucy fell to the mat. As she did, Karen grabbed the back of her bikini top and pulled as hard as she could. The bra ripped apart.

To the cheers of the crowd, Karen held up the yellow bra as a trophy. Lucy was back on her feet now, and it was a wonderful sight. Her naked tits were stunning, the nipples huge and engorged. For a second, Karen thought about how much she wanted them in her mouth; then she realized that this was not her lover but her opponent. She had to defeat this woman; she had to win!

Lucy rushed forward and managed to catch Karen as she tried to step aside. In seconds, she had spun around and put Karen into a headlock. She evened the score by tearing off Karen's green bra before she bounced up and down several times to put pressure on Karen's neck. Then she brought up her knee and cracked Karen's jaw, letting her arms go at the same time.

Karen fell back to the mat heavily. Dazed by the blow, she stayed there for a moment. Lucy rushed at her. Karen ducked down, grabbing Lucy's leg and pulling her down beside her. They grappled furiously on the mat.

Karen got hold of the thong of Lucy's bikini and pulled it hard. The fabric tore into Lucy's cunt, and she cried out in pain as it burned her clit. She struck out, punching Karen several times, but the brunette held on. Then the fabric ripped. Karen fell back, her grip on Lucy's bikini lost. Lucy stood up, completely naked, and the crowd cheered.

She was definitely not a natural blonde; her cunt hairs were thick and dark on her mound, while her pussy was shaved clean. She threw herself at Karen and landed a solid blow. As Karen tried to stand, Lucy kept pulling her down. The two fought desperately on the mat, each trying to gain the upper hand. Karen's bikini ripped as well. Now they were both naked, their skin slippery with sweat. Close to the action, the first rows of women watching also noticed that their cunts were shiny with more than just perspiration.

Karen got to her knees and was just about to get to her feet when Lucy reached up. She got hold of Karen's nipple with a strong right hand and twisted it as hard as she could.

Karen screamed with rage and pain. She was helpless now, unable to react against the agony of having the tender nub squeezed. Lucy smiled cruelly. She grabbed the other nipple and twisted it as well, bringing Karen back to her knees. She used it to guide her opponent, forcing her to move as she wished, leading her with the nipples.

The tables turned when Karen reached under and grabbed her cunt. She took as much flesh as she could and squeezed her fingers together, bringing tears to Lucy's eyes. They were deadlocked together, one with her nipples crushed, the other with her cunt twisted. They brought each other close, neither willing to forfeit, neither able to do anything but inflict pain upon the other even as she tried to ignore her own.

Lucy gave in first, Lucy whose entire body was on fire from the agony in her cunt. She let go of Karen's nipples momentarily. The brunette pulled her huge tits out of Lucy's grasp swiftly, and brought up her other hand to connect solidly with Lucy's jaw.

Lucy went sprawling, but she was back up again almost instantly. They circled each other again, trying to find an opening. The fight was showing on them. They were drenched in sweat, breathing hard. Lucy's lip was swollen, and her arms were bruised. Karen's nipples were puffed and red.

They grabbed each other and grappled again. This time Lucy put out her foot and spun Karen backward over it, using her leg to trip her opponent. Karen fell heavily onto her back and Lucy was on her in a second, striking with her fists and burying her knee in Karen's groin. Karen put up her hands to ward off the blows, grabbing Lucy's wrists. Once again they were deadlocked, but Lucy broke it by pushing down hard with her knee. Karen dropped her hands, trying to push Lucy off her. She succeeded, but only before Lucy slammed her twice more in the temple.

Slash watched them from the sidelines, more than happy with their performance and with the way the crowd was cheering them on. Her own boxer shorts were wet with the juice from her throbbing cunt; her nipples were hard and so swollen with desire that the rings couldn't move in their holes. She loved pinup-type girls, the exaggerated femininity, the globular tits, the perfect hair. She loved them even more when they were like these two, brawling like common sluts.

They were both tired now, and their reactions weren't as razor sharp. Lucy tried to move away, to stand back and grab an opening, but Karen caught her ankle and pulled her back. Her hand slipped on the sweaty skin. She was on top of Lucy in a second, holding her wrists down on the mat. They stayed like that for several moments, both of them seemingly in agreement to just catch their breath. Their tits were touching, the nipples brushing against each other. The audience let out another cheer as they did.

Then the moment passed; the fighters gathered their strength. Lucy struggled under Karen's body, lifting her hips in an effort to buck Karen off. The brunette fell forward so that her tits were right in Lucy's face. Lucy opened her mouth and bit Karen's breast hard; the brunette screamed and hit Lucy repeatedly in the face until she let go her grip. The blonde gathered her energy and pushed. She knocked Karen away; the brunette fell heavily to the mat.

Still dazed from the blows, Lucy was showing the worst of it. Karen got up quickly, spun around, and threw herself over her opponent. Lucy kicked at her, knocking her away, and jumped to her feet again. This time, though, Karen was ready for her. Lucy took a run at her, but at the last moment, Karen stepped aside and thrust out her leg, pushing Lucy at the same time. The blonde fell heavily into the ropes. Karen grabbed her by the hair, pulling her head back, and knocked her repeatedly into the thick ropes. She then took the handful of hair and banged Lucy's forehead into the ropes; when she let go, Lucy fell to the mat with a thud and stayed there.

Karen circled warily, a fist raised, waiting for Lucy to get up. But the blonde was finished, too punished to carry on. Slowly, after several moments, she raised a hand weakly in defeat. The fight was over.

Even as she walked toward the ring, Slash had the microphone in her hand and was already announcing the winner. Around her, it was easy to see who had bet on Karen by their loud cheers. Even more than the bets won, though, it was obvious that every woman in the room was turned on, her cunt throbbing with desire. The sight of these two gorgeous woman wrestling with each other had aroused them.

Slash mounted the stairs, about to slip between the ropes and announce the winner. Lucy was still on the mat, naked, her legs slightly open, her bruised face contorted with anger at knowing she had lost the prize money. Despite her fury, though, it was obvious that her cunt was juicy with desire.

Before Slash could get into the ring, Karen was on her knees in front of her defeated opponent. To the renewed cheers of the crowd, the brunette, who simply couldn't wait another moment, bent down and took Lucy's shaved pussy between her lips.

She was starving with her desire to eat another woman's pussy, and Lucy's luscious body, so like her own, turned her on. The fight had heightened her desire so that her own cunt was pulsating with a beat of its own. She lapped the hot juice from Lucy's hairless cunt and then pushed her tongue as far as she could into Lucy's hole.

Most of the women in the crowd kept their eyes on the two women in the ring, in the glare of the hot white light, but Slash could also see in the background that several had paired off. A number of women were getting their cunts sucked out as Karen did the same in the ring. Slash held back; she would let this scene run its course. Hey, a fight and then a public licking! Who said you couldn't have it all? Lucy had composed herself and now realized, to her delight, that there was an expert tongue between her cuntlips. She looked up and, for a moment, was furious to discover that it was the woman who had beaten her, who had shamed her publicly. But the hot sensations from her cunt overcame her fury quickly, and in a moment she was sighing with pleasure and lifting her hips up so that Karen could get a better angle at her clit. Her own mouth was watering for want of a cunt, so she said, "Bring yours around here, honey. There's no use only one of us getting it." Karen complied immediately.

A throaty cheer went up from the crowd again. A sixty-nine on the floor of the ring! The two fighters hardly heard it. All that mattered was pussy. Karen bent over and fucked Lucy's hole with her tongue while Lucy pulled Karen's perfect asscheeks down so that she could bury her face in the hot, juicy slit and lick out the nectar that ran over her chin.

They were so hot that each touch was electric, a current that ran through their bodies. They were moaning and bucking so hard that it was difficult for them to keep their mouths on each other. Lucy reached up and inserted two fingers into Karen's soaked tunnel, fucking her with her hand while her tongue played over the huge clit. Karen held Lucy's thighs, pulling her into her mouth, onto her tongue with hard, sharp thrusts. Each thrust jerked Lucy's whole body, pushing her tongue deeper into Karen's gash. They wanted to crawl into each other, to get their whole bodies deep into each other's pussies.

They were fucking and sucking in silence, too involved now even to moan their pleasure. Several women in the front row watching them were feeling their own cunts, so excited that most of them didn't even realize they were doing it. Mistresses were ordering submissives to drop to the floor, lifting their skirts or dropping their pants, presenting their soaked cunts to be pleasured. Couples were fingering each other, wanting to suck their lover's cunt, but unwilling to take their eyes away from the spectacle on the mat of the boxing ring. This was just too hot to miss!

Her trembling indicated that Lucy was about to come. Karen kept fucking her with her tongue, at the same time rubbing the hard button of Lucy's clit with her fingertip. Her hand was a blur as she pushed the clit back and forth, and her head moved like a jackhammer, pounding her tongue inside. With a cry that could be heard in every corner of the bar, Lucy climaxed, her whole body trembling, her hips bucking so hard that Karen could barely stay on top.

Lucy let the orgasm wash over her, and then returned immediately to Karen's cunt. She could feel the clit growing on her tongue, getting harder in response to her movements on it. Her face was soaked with saliva and pussyjuice; her fingers were sticky with it, deep in Karen's hole. She pulled Karen so hard into her that she could hardly breathe. Her mouth, her nose, her whole face was surrounded by pussy. She had cunt on her cheeks, her lips; she had cunt on her eyes; she was buried in cunt. She gave a final lick and then, as hard as she could, sucked Karen's clit into her mouth.

It was just the movement that Karen needed. She sat straight up on Lucy's face, bucking her hips, grinding her cunt in as hard as she possibly could. She couldn't get enough of it, and she rode it out, trying to reach the last final movement that would put her over. She stayed on the edge for more than a minute, gasping, moaning, her huge tits heaving, her mouth open in ecstasy. The pressure in her belly was so intense that she could hardly stand it. She needed to come; she had to come! She was so close, so close, she would die if she didn't peak and go over. She had to come—and then Lucy drove her fingers deep into Karen's cunt and sucked her clit between her lips, holding it firmly while her tongue stabbed against it again and again.

That was what she needed. Karen cried out, moaning louder and louder, and then screamed her pleasure as the pressure in her belly broke and she came. She ground on Lucy's mouth, trying to put her whole cunt inside. Wave after wave went through her, until she was dizzy with sex. Then there was a final body-splitting tremor that left her drained.

No longer opponents but lovers, the two of them fell together on the mat in a mutual gesture of complete satisfaction. Their faces battered, their bodies bruised, they had passed over the undefined and unexplained line between pain and pleasure, having found that one could very easily lead to the other.

The crowd thinned out a bit; the show finished, they gave their attention over to their lovers or to strangers, now needful, now wanting to eat or be eaten, to quench the fire that had been stoked by the fighters in the ring.

There was no further announcement of the winner; after a while, when they had composed themselves, the two women left the ring, picked up their discarded robes and walked back to the office where they had left their clothes.

Walking back through the room, Ramone stopped Stef as she rushed by with a tray of drinks. The lack of pomp and showmanship following the fight surprised her; her friend normally reveled in it. "Where did Slash go?"

Stef grinned. "It seems the floor show affects just about everyone," she said and pointed to the bar.

Slash was behind it, and for a moment Ramone was completely confused; it just wasn't like Slash to leave the spotlight during the floor show to come back to pour drinks. But as she got closer, she saw Slash's expression, and she realized exactly what was going on. It became even clearer when her friend shivered and moaned, closed her eyes, and then trembled hard. She stayed like that for a long time and then said something. Ramone had to grin as Cherry popped into view from behind the bar, licking her lips to get every last bit of Slash's pussyjuice from her mouth.

"Couldn't wait?" she teased as she came back behind the bar.

"Oh, not for another second," Slash said as she adjusted the satin boxers and started to reach for a glass. "Who could, after watching something like that?"

"Not too many of them, if the floor's any indication," Ramone said. "I don't think there's a table out there that doesn't have a woman stretched across it with another one between her legs! This is definitely the type of entertainment we'll have to set up again."

"Without a doubt," Slash said. "But fuck, if only I'd known!"

"Known what?"

"That those sluts were going to do that," Slash said, only half in jest. "I should have just told them that the winner got first dibs on going down on the other one. I could have saved myself ten thousand dollars and still got exactly the same action out of them."

Ramone reached up and kissed her hard, running a finger across the thin gold chain that connected Slash's nipple rings. "Tell them that the winner gets to go down on you. Never mind a fight—those bitches would kill each other for a prize like that!"

Chapter Twelve

Slash opened the huge steel front door of Rough Trade and slipped outside, onto the empty sidewalk.

She stood there in front of the bar and just looked around, just listened. To the east, the sky was beginning to lighten, although a sliver of the moon was still out. The city was relatively quiet, beginning to come to life, to get ready for the rush hour. Slash loved being at complete odds with most of the city. As they were winding down for the evening, she was just starting her day. When they slept, she partied in the bar, reveling in the noise, the crowd, the action. When the bleary-eyed workers were stumbling from their apartments and reaching for their morning coffee, she was wide awake in her apartment, debating whether to go to bed, or to squeeze in some last-minute activities. They lived by the sun; she lived by the moon.

The air was cool and damp on her bare legs, for she still wore her satin boxer shorts. She pulled the green satin jacket around her, leaving it open just enough that she could look down and see the gold chain that stretched between her nipples.

The street was empty, save for the occasional taxi or police car that went by. None of the drivers even glanced at her. She loved New York at this time of the morning, when it seemed as if she was the only person who was really at ease with herself, completely awake, completely in tune.

She heard the heavy door open behind her, and Ramone stepped outside with her. "Whatcha doing?" the Japanese woman asked.

"Nothing at all." Slash smiled. "Want to do it with me?" Her friend came to stand beside her and they both just looked around for a long time, watching the rising sun paint patterns on the windows of the office towers.

"We had a good night," Ramone said. "I just finished balancing the till. I don't think we've pulled down that much since the night you staged the fisting."

"Well, the strength of the fight tonight ought to carry us for quite a while," Slash said. "Once the stories start to make their way around the city, we'll be that busy every night of the week. When it starts to go back to normal, I'll think of something else. What outrageous thing haven't we done yet?"

Ramone laughed. "I don't think there's anything we haven't done. And if there is, I'm sure you'll come up with it."

Slash looked around again, this time at the front of the building. "Did you ever think we'd get to this point?"

"Never in a million years," Ramone said. "I remember

the day you asked me to come and work for you, and when I said yes and quit my job, I went home and thought about it, convinced I'd lost my mind."

"So did everyone else," Slash said. "I'd been open only about a week at that point. Remember how most nights we used to sit and pour each other glasses of beer so we wouldn't forget how to do it if a real customer came in?" She laughed. "I was sure I was going down in flames and taking you with me, and I felt bad about that. I was sure they were going to come and padlock the door at any time."

"But they didn't," Ramone said. "You persevered. Now look how far you've come."

"How far *we've* come," Slash corrected her. She put a hand around Ramone's shoulders and drew her close; they stood on the sidewalk together, arms about each other. "My best friend helped me every inch of the way. Don't ever forget that."

She bent down and kissed the Japanese woman on the lips. Standing here in front of her bar, on the New York City sidewalk as the sun came up, it was the perfect ending to a spectacular night.

"Feel like going inside?" Ramone asked.

"I could stand out here all morning, if it stayed just like this," Slash said. "I love being outside at this hour. But only if I don't have a counteroffer like that."

They went back through the heavy steel door, and Slash locked it from the inside. It would remain that way until the evening, when Slash would unlock it and open it to the line of women that would begin to form an hour before opening time. It was the hottest lesbian bar in North America; the days of waiting for customers would never come again.

In anticipation, Ramone had already shed her clothes,

and Slash admired her from across the room before she joined her friend at the bar. This was where they worked all night, where they felt the most comfortable.

Slash went to her. They stood together and looked at the boxing ring. The lights were still on it, and the canvas glowed bright white under them. "That was some battle," the black woman said.

"I love to watch women wrestling," Ramone admitted.

"Well, it sure turned me on." Slash slipped off the satin jacket and tossed it onto a bar stool. "Can I show you how much?"

She slipped out of the satin boxer shorts, leaving on the heavy wrestling boots, and took Ramone into her arms. Their lips met as gently as a whisper, but that changed quickly as both of them grew excited at the touch. Within moments, their gentle kiss was a hungry one, their tongues deep in each other's mouths.

Slash sat down on a bar stool, lifting up her knee. Ramone straddled it, her pussy hot and wet on the skin of Slash's leg. The Japanese woman reached for Slash's nipples and touched the rings ever so gently. Slash groaned.

"Does it hurt?" Ramone asked.

Slash shivered. "They're just a little tender. But it feels so good! One second it hurts, the next it feels like you've got your mouth all over them. I love the way it goes back and forth. Please play with them—they're yours."

Ramone did. She ran her fingers all around them, tracing circles on the breast skin around the nipples, and then she put a fingernail through each ring and tugged on it so gently that the skin barely moved. She ran her finger back and forth across the gold chain that bound the rings together. Then she bent down and took each nipple into her mouth; Slash groaned aloud with delight as she did. The hot wetness was fabulous. Ramone licked around each once and then flipped the rings with her tongue while they were in her mouth. Slash looked down; the sight of her friend with the chocolate-brown tits in her mouth, the gold chain gleaming on her lips, made Slash's cunt run hot and wet.

"Now fuck my leg," Slash said. Ramone sat back, her hands on Slash's shoulders, her pussy firmly on Slash's leg. She moved her hips slowly and smoothly, back and forth, while her cunt rubbed on Slash's skin.

They bent toward each other and kissed passionately while Ramone kept up her movement. Slash could feel the wetness on her leg. She ran her finger through it and then pressed it on Ramone's lip. Ramone tasted her own cunt on her mouth; she savored it, and then went back to Slash's lips for another deep kiss.

Slash's hands moved to Ramone's tits, to their exquisite firmness and their oversized nipples. Ramone kept her own hands on Slash's shoulders to keep her balance. She groaned as Slash played with her breasts. She looked down; she loved the sight of Slash's dark hands on her own olive skin. When Slash leaned forward and took one of the tits into her mouth, Ramone groaned and hurried up her movements on Slash's leg.

The empty bar echoed with the noises they made. The wooden bar stool creaked with the fevered motion as Ramone, now desperate to come, slid and pounded on Slash's leg. Slash's hands were all over Ramone—one on her tit, another on her own leg where Ramone was sliding. Each time Ramone's cunt came close, her clit slid up over Slash's finger and rubbed on it. Ramone moaned each time this extra pressure came onto her swollen nub.

Her orgasm was so strong that it took her by surprise. Once again the huge room echoed, this time with the sound of her cries. She banged her cunt against Slash, against Slash's hand, against her leg. Both of them were soaked with pussyjuice, hot with needy cunt. Both of them cried in ecstasy as Ramone came.

When it was all over, she relaxed on Slash's leg, completely satisfied with her own orgasm. But it was not enough; she slipped off her friend's leg, fell to her knees, and pushed Slash's legs apart.

She loved the taste of Slash's cunt so much she could have stayed there forever. She buried her tongue deep into the wet folds, taking great delight in Slash's moans as she did. She knew exactly where to lick, where to thrust her tongue. She knew the movements, knew when to speed up, when to slow down. She and Slash fit together perfectly, and this was their proof.

The thick cuntjuice covered her lips and chin as she licked and sucked. She took it into her, filled her mouth with it. She wished there was enough of it to drink. Had she been able to drown in it, she would have died happily.

Meanwhile, Slash was giving herself over to her passion, allowing herself to fall into it. The pressure was building up, and she was thrilled to be able to let herself go with Ramone. Any restraint she might have shown with any other woman was never shown with Ramone. She gave herself up; she let herself shout; she let Ramone know exactly how good it felt. With Ramone she was always herself.

Now it was time to let Ramone know again. Slash could feel the climax building to its peak each time Ramone flashed her tongue over the sensitive ruby-red clit. Her pussy was so swollen with sex that it felt like it might explode. Ramone licked it harder, harder, and then stayed right on the tip of her clit. Her tongue moved over it like a blur.

That was all Slash needed. The pressure broke like water behind a dam, carrying her with it. She cried out to the empty room, a series of quick moans that dissolved into a long-drawn-out cry of pleasure. Ramone stayed with her until it was all over and then, with long, slow laps of her tongue, she cleaned up the last of the pussyjuice, savoring its flavor in her mouth.

"You always know exactly how to do me," Slash gasped as she tried to catch her breath. Ramone got up from the floor and sat on the bar stool next to her.

"That's from so many years of eating that wonderful pussy," Ramone said. "Everyone gets better with practice. Unlike people who have to learn how to play the piano, though, I love recitals!"

Slash reached over and picked up the satin jacket from the other stool. "I think we've been in this bar long enough for one day," she said. "Time to close up. What do you think?"

"Well, it's certainly been a day to remember." Ramone reached for her clothes.

"Going home?"

"Got a better suggestion?"

Slash pulled on the jacket and smiled at her friend. "The morning is still young, and so are we. I'd be a lot happier if you'd come upstairs and spend the rest of it with me."

Ramone got up off the stool and waited while Slash went behind the bar and turned off all but a single bank of lights, which she left on for security. Then the two of them, arm in arm, walked through the huge, silent bar, their footsteps echoing through the room.

"Hard to believe that in less than ten hours, you won't be able to move three steps in any direction, or be able to hear anyone who isn't shouting," Ramone said.

Slash agreed. "It is, but that's ten hours from now. Considering what you and I can do to each other in ten hours, I'd call it more like an eternity."

MASQUERADE

JENNIFER AGAIN
$4.95/220-5
An incendiary sequel chronicling the exploits of one of modern erotica's most famous heroines. Once again, the insatiable Jennifer seizes the day—and extracts from it every last drop of sensual pleasure! No man is immune to this vixen's charms.

JENNIFER
$4.95/107-1
From the bedroom of a notoriously insatiable dancer to an uninhibited ashram, *Jennifer* traces the exploits of one thoroughly modern woman as she lustfully explores the limits of her own sexuality.

THE ROMANCES OF BLANCHE LA MARE
$4.95/101-2
When Blanche loses her husband, it becomes clear she'll need a job. She sets her sights on the stage—and soon encounters a cast of lecherous characters intent on making her path to suckess as hot and hard as possible!

PETER JASON
WAYWARD
$4.95/3004-0
A mysterious countess hires a tour bus for an unusual vacation. Traveling through Europe's most notorious cities, she picks up friends, lovers, and acquaintances from every walk of life in pursuit of pleasure.

RHINOCEROS

GERI NETTICK WITH BETH ELLIOT
MIRRORS:
PORTRAIT OF A LESBIAN TRANSSEXUAL
$6.95/435-6
The alternately heartbreaking and empowering story of one woman's long road to full selfhood. Born a male, Geri Nettick knew something just didn't fit. And even after coming to terms with her own gender dysphoria—and taking steps to correct it—she still fought to be accepted by the lesbian feminist community to which she felt she belonged. A fascinating, true tale of struggle and discovery.

TRISTAN TAORMINO
& DAVID AARON CLARK, EDITORS
RITUAL SEX
$6.95/391-0
While many people believe the body and soul to occupy almost completely independent realms, the many contributors to *Ritual Sex* know—and demonstrate—that the two share more common ground than society feels comfortable acknowledging. From personal memoirs of ecstatic revelation, to fictional quests to reconcile sex and spirit, *Ritual Sex* delves into forbidden areas with gusto, providing an unprecedented look at private life. Includes work by such legendary erotic pioneers as Terence Sellers, Genesis P-Orridge, Guy Baldwin, Kate Bornstein, Annie Sprinkle, Mark Thompson, and many more.

TAMMY JO ECKHART
PUNISHMENT FOR THE CRIME
$6.95/427-5
Peopled by characters of rare depth, these stories explore the true meaning of dominance and submission, and offer some surprising revelations. From an encounter between two of society's most despised individuals, to the explorations of longtime friends, these tales take you where few others have ever dared....

THOMAS S. ROCHE, EDITOR
NOIROTICA:
AN ANTH. OF EROTIC CRIME STORIES
$6.95/390-2
A collection of darkly sexy tales, taking place at the crossroads of the crime and erotic genres. Thomas S. Roche has gathered together some of today's finest writers of sexual fiction, all of whom explore the murky terrain where desire runs irrevocably afoul of the law.

DAVID MELTZER
UNDER
$6.95/290-6
The story of a sex professional living at the bottom of the social heap. After surgeries designed to increase his physical allure, corrupt government forces drive the cyber-gigolo underground—where even more bizarre cultures await him.

THE LOVING DOMINANT
$6.95/218-3
Everything you need to know about an infamous sexual variation—and an unspoken type of love. Mentor—a longtime player in scene—guides readers through this world and reveals the too-often hidden basis of the D/S relationship: care, trust and love.

GARY BOWEN
DIARY OF A VAMPIRE
$6.95/331-7
"Gifted with a darkly sensual vision and a fresh voice, [Bowen] is a writer to watch out for." —Cecilia Tan
The chilling, arousing, and ultimately moving memoirs of an undead—but all too human—soul. Bowen's Rafael, a red-blooded male with an insatiable hunger for the same, is the perfect antidote to the effete malcontents haunting bookstores today. *Diary of a Vampire* marks the emergence of a bold and brilliant vision, firmly rooted in past and present.

GRANT ANTREWS
MY DARLING DOMINATRIX
$6.95/447-X
When a man and a woman fall in love, it's supposed to be simple, uncomplicated, easy—unless that woman happens to be a dominatrix. Curiosity gives way to unblushing desire in this story of one man's awakening to the joys of willing slavery.

LAURA ANTONIOU WRITING AS "SARA ADAMSON"
THE TRAINER
$6.95/249-3
The Marketplace—the ultimate underground sexual realm includes not only willing slaves, but the exquisite trainers who take submissives firmly in hand. And now these mentors divulge the desires that led them to become the ultimate figures of authority.
THE SLAVE
$6.95/173-X
This second volume in the "Marketplace" trilogy further elaborates the world of slaves and masters. One talented submissive longs to join the ranks of those who have proven themselves worthy of entry into the Marketplace. But the delicious price is staggeringly high....

THE MARKETPLACE
$6.95/3096-2
"Merchandise does not come easily to the Marketplace.... They haunt the clubs and the organizations.... Some are so ripe that they intimidate the poseurs, the weekend sadists and the furtive dilettantes who are so endemic to that world. And they never stop asking where we may be found...."

DAVID AARON CLARK
SISTER RADIANCE
$6.95/215-9
A chronicle of a most desperate obsession—rife with Clark's trademark vivisections of contemporary desires, sacred and profane. The vicissitudes of lust and romance are examined against a backdrop of urban decay and shallow fashionability in this testament to the allure—and inevitability—of the forbidden.
THE WET FOREVER
$6.95/117-9
The story of Janus and Madchen—a small-time hood and a beautiful sex worker on the run from one of the most dangerous men they have ever known—*The Wet Forever* examines themes of loyalty, sacrifice, redemption and obsession amidst Manhattan's sex parlors and underground S/M clubs. Its combination of sex and suspense led Terence Sellers to proclaim it "evocative and poetic."

ALICE JOANOU
BLACK TONGUE
$6.95/258-2
"Joanou has created a series of sumptuous, brooding, dark visions of sexual obsession, and is undoubtedly a name to look out for in the future." —*Redeemer*
Exploring lust at its most florid and unsparing, *Black Tongue* is a trove of baroque fantasies—each redolent of forbidden passions. Joanou creates some of erotica's most mesmerizing and unforgettable characters.
TOURNIQUET
$6.95/3060-1
A heady collection of stories and effusions from the pen of one our most dazzling young writers. Strange tales abound, from the story of the mysterious and cruel Cybele, to an encounter with the sadistic entertainment of a bizarre after-hours cafe. A complex and riveting series of meditations on desire.

MASQUERADE DIRECT

RHINOCEROS

CANNIBAL FLOWER
$4.95/72-6

The provocative debut volume from this acclaimed writer. "She is waiting in her darkened bedroom, as she has waited throughout history, to seduce the men who are foolish enough to be blinded by her irresistible charms.... She is the goddess of sexuality, and *Cannibal Flower* is her haunting siren song."
—Michael Perkins

MICHAEL PERKINS
EVIL COMPANIONS
$6.95/3067-9

Set in New York City during the tumultuous waning years of the Sixties, *Evil Companions* has been hailed as "a frightening classic." A young couple explores the nether reaches of the erotic unconscious in a shocking confrontation with the extremes of passion. With a new introduction by science fiction legend Samuel R. Delany.

AN ANTHOLOGY OF CLASSIC ANONYMOUS EROTIC WRITING
$6.95/140-3

Michael Perkins has collected the very best passages from the world's erotic writing. "Anonymous" is one of the most infamous bylines in publishing history —and these steamy excerpts show why! An incredible smorgasbord of forbidden delights culled from some of the most famous titles in the history of erotic literature.

THE SECRET RECORD: MODERN EROTIC LITERATURE
$6.95/3039-3

Michael Perkins surveys the field with authority and unique insight. Updated and revised to include the latest trends, tastes, and developments in this misunderstood and maligned genre.

HELEN HENLEY
ENTER WITH TRUMPETS
$6.95/197-7

Helen Henley was told that women just don't write about sex—much less the taboos she was so interested in exploring. So Henley did it alone, flying in the face of "tradition," by writing this touching tale of arousal and devotion in one couple's kinky relationship.

PHILIP JOSÉ FARMER
FLESH
$6.95/303-1

Space Commander Stagg explored the galaxies for 800 years. Upon his return, the hero Stagg, hoped to be afforded a hero's welcome. Once home, he is made the centerpiece of an incredible public ritual—one that will repeatedly take him to the heights of ecstasy, and inexorably drag him toward the depths of hell.

A FEAST UNKNOWN
$6.95/276-0

"Sprawling, brawling, shocking, suspenseful, hilarious..."
—Theodore Sturgeon

Farmer's supreme anti-hero returns. "I was conceived and born in 1888." Slowly, Lord Grandrith—armed with the belief that he is the son of Jack the Ripper—tells the story of his remarkable and unbridled life. His story begins with his discovery of the secret of immortality—and progresses to encompass the furthest extremes of human behavior. A classic of speculative erotica—and proof of Farmer's long-admired genius.

THE IMAGE OF THE BEAST
$6.95/166-7

Herald Childe has seen Hell, glimpsed its horror in an act of sexual mutilation. Childe must now find and destroy an inhuman predator through the streets of a polluted and decadent Los Angeles of the future. One clue after another leads Childe to an inescapable realization about the nature of sex and evil....

LEOPOLD VON SACHER-MASOCH
VENUS IN FURS
$6.95/3089-X

This classic 19th century novel is the first uncompromising exploration of the dominant/submissive relationship in literature. The alliance of Severin and Wanda epitomizes Sacher-Masoch's dark obsession with a cruel, controlling goddess and the urges that drive the man held in her thrall. This special edition includes the letters exchanged between Sacher-Masoch and Emilie Mataja, an aspiring writer he sought to cast as the avatar of the forbidden desires expressed in his most famous work.

RHINOCEROS

SAMUEL R. DELANY
THE MAD MAN
$8.99/408-9

"The latest novel from Hugo- and Nebula-winning science fiction writer and critic Delany...reads like a pornographic reflection of Peter Ackroyd's *Chatterton* or A. S. Byatt's *Possession*.... The pornographic element... becomes more than simple shock or titillation, though, as Delany develops an insightful dichotomy between [his protagonist]'s two worlds: the one of cerebral philosophy and dry academia, the other of heedless, 'impersonal' obsessive sexual extremism. When these worlds finally collide...the novel achieves a surprisingly satisfying resolution...." —*Publishers Weekly*

The mass market debut of Samuel R. Delany's most provocative novel. For his thesis, graduate student John Marr researches the life and work of the brilliant Timothy Hasler: a philosopher whose career was cut tragically short over a decade earlier. On another front, Marr finds himself increasingly drawn toward more shocking, depraved sexual entanglements with the homeless men of his neighborhood, until it begins to seem that Hasler's death might hold some key to his own life as a gay man in the age of AIDS. An acclaimed examination of the outer boundaries of human desire.

EQUINOX
$6.95/157-8

The Scorpion has sailed the seas in a quest for every possible pleasure. Her crew is a collection of the young, the twisted, the insatiable. A drifter comes into their midst and is taken on a fantastic journey to the darkest, most dangerous sexual extremes—until he is finally a victim to their boundless appetites. The novel that paved the way for the frank explorations of *The Mad Man*, *Equinox* (originally published as *The Tides of Lust*) finally returns to print

SOPHIE GALLEYMORE BIRD
MANEATER
$6.95/103-9

Through a bizarre act of creation, a man attains the "perfect" lover—by all appearances a beautiful, sensuous woman, but in reality something far darker. Once brought to life she will accept no mate, seeking instead the prey that will sate her hunger for vengeance. A biting take on the war of the sexes, this debut goes for the jugular of the "perfect woman" myth.

TUPPY OWENS
SENSATIONS
$6.95/3081-4

Tuppy Owens tells the unexpurgated story of the making of *Sensations*—the first big-budget sex flick. Originally commissioned to appear in book form after the release of the film in 1975, *Sensations* is finally released under Masquerade's stylish Rhinoceros imprint.

DANIEL VIAN
ILLUSIONS
$6.95/3074-1

Two tales of danger and desire in Berlin on the eve of WWII. From private homes to lurid cafés, passion is exposed and explored in stark contrast to the brutal violence of the time. A singularly arousing volume; two sexy tales examining a remarkably decadent age.

PERSUASIONS
$6.95/183-7

"The stockings are drawn tight by the suspender belt, tight enough to be stretched to the limit just above the middle part of her thighs..." A double novel, including the classics *Adagio* and *Gabriela and the General*, this volume traces desire around the globe. Two classics of international lust!

ANDREI CODRESCU
THE REPENTANCE OF LORRAINE
$6.95/329-5

"One of our most prodigiously talented and magical writers." —*NYT Book Review*

By the acclaimed author of *The Hole in the Flag* and *The Blood Countess*. An aspiring writer, a professor's wife, a secretary, gold anklets, Maoists, Roman harlots—and more—swirl through this spicy tale of a harried quest for a mythic artifact. Written when the author was a young man, this lusty yarn was inspired by the heady days of the Sixties.

LIESEL KULIG
LOVE IN WARTIME
$6.95/3044-X

Madeleine knew that the handsome SS officer was a dangerous man, but she was just a cabaret singer in Nazi-occupied Paris, trying to survive in a perilous time. When Josef fell in love with her, he discovered that a beautiful and amoral woman can sometimes be more dangerous than a highly skilled soldier.

DIRECT

BADBOY

THE CITADEL
$4.95/198-5
The sequel to The Initiation of PB 500. Having proven himself worthy of his stunning master, Micah—now known only as "500"—will face new challenges and hardships after his entry into the forbidding Citadel. Only his master knows what awaits—and whether Micah will again distinguish himself as the perfect instrument of pleasure....

RITUALS
$4.95/168-3
Via a computer bulletin board, a young man finds himself drawn into a series of sexual rites that transform him into the willing slave of a mysterious stranger. Gradually, all vestiges of his former life are thrown off, and he learns to live for his Master's touch....

THE INITIATION PB 500
$4.95/141-1
An interstellar accident strands a young stud on an alien planet. He is a stranger on their planet, unschooled in their language, and ignorant of their customs. But this man, Micah—now known only by his number—will soon be trained in every last detail of erotic personal service. And, once nurtured and transformed into the perfect physical specimen, he must begin proving himself worthy of the master who has chosen him....

ROBERT BAHR

SEX SHOW
$4.95/225-6
Luscious dancing boys. Brazen, explicit acts. Unending stimulation. Take a seat, and get very comfortable, because the curtain's going up on a show no discriminating appetite can afford to miss.

"BIG" BILL JACKSON

EIGHTH WONDER
$4.95/200-0
From the bright lights and back rooms of New York to the open fields and sweaty bods of a small Southern town, "Big" Bill always manages to cause a scene, and the more actors he can involve, the better! Like the man's name says, he's got more than enough for everyone, and turns nobody down....

JASON FURY

THE ROPE ABOVE, THE BED BELOW
$4.95/269-8
The irresistible Jason Fury returns—and if you thought his earlier adventures were hot, this volume will blow you away! Once again, our built, blond hero finds himself in the oddest—and most compromising—positions.

ERIC'S BODY
$4.95/151-9
Meet Jason Fury—blond, blue-eyed and up for anything. Fury's sexiest tales are collected in book form for the first time. Follow the irresistible Jason through sexual adventures unlike any you have ever read....

JOHN ROWBERRY

LEWD CONDUCT
$4.95/3091-1
Flesh-and-blood men vie for power, pleasure and surrender in each of these feverish stories, and no one walks away from his steamy encounter unsated. Rowberry's men are unafraid to push the limits of civilized behavior in search of the elusive and empowering conquest.

LARS EIGHNER

WHISPERED IN THE DARK
$5.95/286-8
A volume demonstrating Eighner's unique combination of strengths: poetic descriptive power, an unfailing ear for dialogue, and a finely tuned feeling for the nuances of male passion.

AMERICAN PRELUDE
$4.95/170-5
Eighner is widely recognized as one of our best, most exciting gay writers. He is also one of gay erotica's true masters—and American Prelude shows why. Wonderfully written, blisteringly hot tales of all-American lust.

BADBOY

B.M.O.C.
$4.95/3077-6

In a college town known as "the Athens of the Southwest," studs of every stripe are up all night—studying, naturally. In *B.M.O.C.*, Lars Eighner includes the very best of his short stories, sure to appeal to the collegian in every man. Relive university life the way it was supposed to be, with a cast of handsome honor students majoring in Human Homosexuality.

CALDWELL/EIGHNER
QSFX2
$5.95/278-7

The wickedest, wildest, other-worldliest yarns from two master storytellers—Clay Caldwell and Lars Eighner. Both eroticists take a trip to the furthest reaches of the sexual imagination, sending back ten stories proving that as much as things change, one thing will always remain the same....

JR
FRENCH QUARTER NIGHTS
$5.95/337-6

A randy roundup of this author's most popular tales. *French Quarter Nights* is filled with sensual snapshots of the many places where men get down and dirty—from the steamy French Quarter to the steam room at the old Everard baths. In the best tradition of gay erotica, these are nights you'll wish would go on forever....

AARON TRAVIS
IN THE BLOOD
$5.95/283-3

Written when Travis had just begun to explore the true power of the erotic imagination, these stories laid the groundwork for later masterpieces. Among the many rewarding rarities included in this volume: "In the Blood"—a heart-pounding descent into sexual vampirism, written with the furious erotic power that has distinguished Travis' work from the beginning.

THE FLESH FABLES
$4.95/243-4

One of Travis' best collections, finally rereleased. *The Flesh Fables* includes "Blue Light," his most famous story, as well as other masterpieces that established him as the erotic writer to watch. And watch carefully, because Travis always buries a surprise somewhere beneath his scorching detail....

SLAVES OF THE EMPIRE
$4.95/3054-7

The return of an undisputed classic from this master of the erotic genre.

"*Slaves of the Empire* is a wonderful mythic tale. Set against the backdrop of the exotic and powerful Roman Empire, this wonderfully written novel explores the timeless questions of light and dark in male sexuality. Travis has shown himself expert in manipulating the most primal themes and images. The locale may be the ancient world, but these are the slaves and masters of our time...."
—John Preston

BIG SHOTS
$5.95/448-8

Two fierce tales in one electrifying volume. In *Beirut*, Travis tells the story of ultimate military power and erotic subjugation; *Kip*, Travis' hypersexed and sinister take on film noir, appears in unexpurgated form for the first time—including the final, overwhelming chapter. Relentless acts and relentless passions dominate these chronicles of unimaginable lust. One of the rawest titles we've ever published.

EXPOSED
$4.95/126-8

A volume of shorter Travis tales, each providing a unique glimpse of the horny gay male in his natural environment! Cops, college jocks, ancient Romans—even Sherlock Holmes and his loyal Watson—cruise these pages, fresh from the throbbing pen of one of our hottest authors.

BEAST OF BURDEN
$4.95/105-5

Five ferocious tales. Innocents surrender to the brutal sexual mastery of their superiors, as taboos are shattered and replaced with the unwritten rules of masculine conquest. Intense, extreme—and totally Travis.

CLAY CALDWELL
ASK OL' BUDDY
$5.95/346-5

One of Caldwell's most popular novels. Set in the underground SM world, Caldwell takes you on a journey of discovery—where men initiate one another into the secrets of the rawest sexual realm of all. And when each stud's initiation is complete, he takes his places among the masters—eager to take part in the training of another hungry soul...

BADBOY

VINCE GILMAN
THE SLAVE PRINCE
$4.95/199-3
A runaway royal learns the true meaning of power when he comes under the hand of Korat—a man well-versed in the many ways of subjugating a young man to his relentless sexual appetite.

BOB VICKERY
SKIN DEEP
$4.95/265-5
Talk about "something for everyone!" *Skin Deep* contains so many varied beauties no one will go away unsatisfied. No tantalizing morsel of manflesh is overlooked—or left unexplored! Beauty may be only skin deep, but a handful of beautiful skin is a tempting proposition.

EDITED BY DAVID LAURENTS
WANDERLUST:
HOMOEROTIC TALES OF TRAVEL
$5.95/395-3
A volume dedicated to the special pleasures of faraway places. Gay men have always had a special interest in travel—and not only for the scenic vistas. Wanderlust celebrates the freedom of the open road, and the allure of men who stray from the beaten path....

THE BADBOY BOOK OF EROTIC POETRY
$5.95/382-1
Over fifty of gay literature's biggest talents are here represented by their hottest verse. Erotic poetry has long been the problem child of the literary world—highly creative and provocative, but somehow too frank to be "literature." Both learned and stimulating, *The Badboy Book of Erotic Poetry* restores eros to its rightful place of honor in contemporary gay writing.

JAMES MEDLEY
HUCK AND BILLY
$4.95/245-0
Young love is always the sweetest, always the most sorrowful. Young lust, on the other hand, knows no bounds—and is often the hottest of one's life! Huck and Billy explore the desires that course through their young male bodies, determined to plumb the lusty depths of passion. A sweetly torrid look at the follies of young manhood.

LARRY TOWNSEND
LEATHER AD: S
$5.95/407-0
The second half of Townsend's acclaimed tale of lust through the personals—this time told from a Top's perspective. A simple ad generates many responses, and one man finds himself in the enviable position of putting these studly applicants through their paces.....

LEATHER AD: M
$5.95/380-5
The first of this two-part classic. John's curious about what goes on between the leatherclad men he's fantasized about. He takes out a personal ad, and starts a journey of self-discovery that will leave no part of his life unchanged.

BEWARE THE GOD WHO SMILES
$5.95/321-X
Two lusty young Americans are transported to ancient Egypt—where they are embroiled in regional warfare and taken as slaves by marauding barbarians. The key to escape from this brutal bondage lies in their own rampant libidos, and urges as old as time itself.

THE CONSTRUCTION WORKER
$5.95/298-1
A young, hung construction worker is sent to a building project in Central America, where he finds that man-to-man sex is the accepted norm. The young stud quickly fits right in — until he senses that beneath the constant sexual shenanigans there moves an almost supernatural force.

2069 TRILOGY
(This one-volume collection only $6.95)244-2
For the first time, Larry Townsend's early science-fiction trilogy appears in one massive volume! Set in a future world, the *2069 Trilogy* includes the tight plotting and shameless male sexual pleasure that established him as one of gay erotica's first masters.

MIND MASTER
$4.95/209-4
Who better to explore the territory of erotic dominance than an author who helped define the genre—and knows that ultimate mastery always transcends the physical.

THE LONG LEATHER CORD
$4.95/201-9
Chuck's stepfather never lacks money or clandestine male visitors with whom he enacts intense sexual rituals. As Chuck comes to terms with his own desires, he begins to unravel the mystery behind his stepfather's secret life.

MASQUERADE DIRECT

BADBOY

MAN SWORD
$4.95/188-8
The tres gai tale of France's King Henri III. Unimaginably spoiled by his mother—the infamous Catherine de Medici—Henri is groomed from a young age to assume the throne of France. Along the way, he encounters enough sexual schemers and randy politicos to alter one's picture of history forever!

THE FAUSTUS CONTRACT
$4.95/167-5
Two attractive young men desperately need $1000. Will do anything. Travel OK. Danger OK. Call anytime... Two cocky young hustlers get more than they bargained for in this story of lust and its discontents.

THE GAY ADVENTURES OF CAPTAIN GOOSE
$4.95/169-1
The hot and tender young Jerome Gander is sentenced to serve aboard the *H.M.S. Faerigold*—a ship manned by the most hardened, unrepentant criminals. In no time, Gander becomes well-versed in the ways of men at sea, and the Faerigold becomes the most notorious ship of its day.

CHAINS
$4.95/158-6
Picking up street punks has always been risky, but in Larry Townsend's classic *Chains*, it sets off a string of events that must be read to be believed. One of Townsend's most remarkable works.

KISS OF LEATHER
$4.95/161-6
A look at the acts and attitudes of an earlier generation of gay leathermen, Kiss of Leather is full to bursting with the gritty, raw action that has distinguished Townsend's work for years. Pain and pleasure mix in this tightly plotted tale.

RUN, LITTLE LEATHER BOY
$4.95/143-8
One young man's sexual awakening. A chronic under-achiever, Wayne seems to be going nowhere fast. When his father puts him to work for a living, Wayne soon finds himself bored with the everyday—and increasingly drawn to the masculine intensity of a dark and mysterious sexual underground....

RUN NO MORE
$4.95/152-7
The continuation of Larry Townsend's legendary *Run, Little Leather Boy*. This volume follows the further adventures of Townsend's leatherclad narrator as he travels every sexual byway available to the S/M male.

THE SCORPIUS EQUATION
$4.95/119-5
Set in the far future, *The Scorpius Equation* is the story of a man caught between the demands of two galactic empires. Our randy hero must match wits—and more—with the incredible forces that rule his world.

THE SEXUAL ADVENTURES OF SHERLOCK HOLMES
$4.95/3097-0
Holmes' most satisfying adventures, from the unexpurgated memoirs of the faithful Mr. Watson. "A Study in Scarlet" is transformed to expose Mrs. Hudson as a man in drag, the Diogenes Club as an S/M arena, and clues only the redoubtable—and very horny—Sherlock Holmes could piece together. A baffling tale of sex and mystery.

FLEDERMAUS

FLEDERFICTION: STORIES OF MEN AND TORTURE
$5.95/355-4
Fifteen blistering paeans to men and their suffering. Fledermaus unleashes his most thrilling tales of punishment in this special volume designed with Badboy readers in mind. No less an authority than Larry Townsend introduces this volume of Fledermaus' best work.

DONALD VINING

CABIN FEVER AND OTHER STORIES
$5.95/338-4
Eighteen blistering stories in celebration of the most intimate of male bonding. Time after time, Donald Vining's men succumb to nature, and reaffirm both love and lust in modern gay life.
Praise for Donald Vining:
"Demonstrates the wisdom experience combined with insight and optimism can create."   —*Bay Area Reporter*

BADBOY

DEREK ADAMS

THE MARK OF THE WOLF
$5.95/361-9

What was happening to me? I didn't understand. I turned to look at the man who stared back at me from the mirror. The familiar outlines of my face seemed coarser, more sinister. An animal? The past comes back to haunt one well-off stud, whose unslakeable thirsts lead him into the arms of many men—and the midst of a perilous mystery.

MY DOUBLE LIFE
$5.95/314-7

Every man leads a double life, dividing his hours between the mundanities of the day and the outrageous pursuits of the night. The creator of sexy P.I. Miles Diamond shines a little light on the wicked things men do when no one's looking.

BOY TOY
$4.95/260-4

Poor Brendan Callan finds himself the guinea pig of a crazed geneticist. The result: Brendan becomes irresistibly alluring—a talent designed for endless pleasure, but coveted by others for the most unsavory means....

HEAT WAVE
$4.95/159-4

"His body was draped in baggy clothes, but there was hardly any doubt that they covered anything less than perfection.... His slacks were cinched tight around a narrow waist, and the rise of flesh pushing against the thin fabric promised a firm, melon-shaped ass...."

MILES DIAMOND AND THE DEMON OF DEATH
$4.95/251-5

Derek Adams' gay gumshoe returns for further adventures. Miles always find himself in the stickiest situations—with any stud whose path he crosses! His adventures with "The Demon of Death" promise another carnal carnival.

THE ADVENTURES OF MILES DIAMOND
$4.95/118-7

The debut of Miles Diamond—Derek Adams' take on the classic American archetype of the hardboiled private eye. "The Case of the Missing Twin" promises to be a most rewarding case, packed as it is with randy studs. Miles sets about uncovering all as he tracks down the elusive and delectable Daniel Travis—all the while indulging himself with the carnal attentions of a host of hot and horny men. As Miles soon discovers, every man has a secret....

KELVIN BELIELE

IF THE SHOE FITS
$4.95/223-X

An essential and winning volume of tales exploring a world where randy boys can't help but do what comes naturally—as often as possible! Sweaty male bodies grapple in pleasure, proving the old adage: if the shoe fits, one might as well slip right in....

VICTOR TERRY

SM/SD
$6.50/406-2

Set around a South Dakota town called Prairie, these tales offer compelling evidence that the real rough stuff can still be found where men roam free of the restraints of "polite" society—and take what they want despite all rules.

WHiPs
$4.95/254-X

Connoisseurs of gay writing have known Victor Terry's work for some time. With *WHiPs*, Terry joins Badboy's roster at last. Cruising for a hot man? You'd better be, because one way or another, these WHiPs—officers of the Wyoming Highway Patrol—are gonna pull you over for a little impromptu interrogation....

MAX EXANDER

DEEDS OF THE NIGHT: TALES OF EROS AND PASSION
$5.95/348-1

MAXimum porn! Exander's a writer who's seen it all—and is more than happy to describe every inch of it in pulsating detail. A whirlwind tour of the hypermasculine libido.

LEATHERSEX
$4.95/210-8

Hard-hitting tales from merciless Max Exander. This time he focuses on the leatherclad lust that draws together only the most willing and talented of tops and bottoms—for an all-out orgy of limitless surrender and control....

MANSEX
$4.95/160-8

"Mark was the classic leatherman: a huge, dark stud in chaps, with a big black moustache, hairy chest and enormous muscles. Exactly the kind of men Todd liked—strong, hunky, masculine, ready to take control...." Rough sex for rugged men.

BADBOY

SEAN MARTIN
SCRAPBOOK
$4.95/224-8

Imagine a book filled with only the best, most vivid remembrances...a book brimming with every hot, sexy encounter its pages can hold... Now you need only open up *Scrapbook* to know that such a volume really exists....

CARO SOLES & STAN TAL, EDITORS
BIZARRE DREAMS
$4.95/187-X

An anthology of stirring voices dedicated to exploring the dark side of human fantasy. *Bizarre Dreams* brings together the most talented practitioners of "dark fantasy," the most forbidden sexual realm of all.

J.A. GUERRA
BADBOY FANTASIES
$4.95/3049-0

When love eludes them—lust will do! Thrill-seeking men caught up in vivid dreams, dark mysteries and brief encounters will keep you gasping throughout these tales.

SLOW BURN
$4.95/3042-3

Welcome to the Body Shoppe, where men's lives cross in the pursuit of muscle. Torsos got lean and hard, pecs widen, and stomachs ripple in these sexy stories of the power and perils of physical perfection.

DAVE KINNICK
SORRY I ASKED
$4.95/3090-3

Unexpurgated interviews with gay porn's rank and file. Get personal with the men behind (and under) the "stars," and discover the hot truth about the porn business.

MICHAEL LOWENTHAL, ED.
THE BADBOY EROTIC LIBRARY VOLUME I
$4.95/190-X

Some of Badboy's biggest successes have been the classic writings of that genius known simply as 'Anonymous.' Discover here the reason so many were forced to pen their work in secret. Excerpts from *A Secret Life, Imre, Sins of the Cities of the Plain, Teleny* and others demonstrate the uncanny gift for portraying sex between men that led to many of these titles being banned upon publication. Available only from Badboy.

THE BADBOY EROTIC LIBRARY VOLUME II
$4.95/211-6

This time, selections are taken from *Mike and Me* and *Muscle Bound, Men at Work, Badboy Fantasies,* and *Slowburn.*

ERIC BOYD
MIKE AND ME
$5.95/419-4

Mike joined the gym squad to bulk up on muscle. Little did he know he'd be turning on every sexy muscle jock in Minnesota! Hard bodies collide in a series of workouts designed to generate a whole lot more than rips and cuts. A nationwide bestseller!

MIKE AND THE MARINES
$5.95/347-3

Mike and Me was one of Badboy's earliest hits, and now readers can revel in another sexy extravaganza. This time, Mike takes on America's most elite corps of studs—running into more than a few good men! Join in on the never-ending sexual escapades of this singularly lustful platoon!

ANONYMOUS
A SECRET LIFE
$4.95/3017-2

Meet Master Charles: only eighteen, and quite innocent, until his arrival at the Sir Percival's Royal Academy, where the daily lessons are supplemented with a crash course in pure, sweet sexual heat! Young men explode with long-suppressed desire!

SINS OF THE CITIES OF THE PLAIN
$5.95/322-8

Victorian prurience—uncensored! Indulge yourself in the scorching memoirs of young man-about-town Jack Saul. With his shocking dalliances with the lords and "ladies" of British high society, Jack's positively sinful escapades grow wilder with every chapter!

IMRE
$4.95/3019-9

What dark secrets, what fiery passions lay hidden behind strikingly beautiful Lieutenant Imre's emerald eyes? An extraordinary lost classic of fantasy, obsession, gay erotic desire, and romance in a small European town on the eve of WWI.

DIRECT

BADBOY

TELENY
$4.95/3020-2
A look at the dark side of Victorian morality. Often attributed to Oscar Wilde, Teleny tells the story of one young man of independent means. He dedicates himself to a succession of forbidden pleasures, but instead finds love and tragedy when he becomes embroiled in a mysterious cult devoted to fulfilling only the very darkest of fantasies. Not to be missed.

PAT CALIFIA
THE SEXPERT
$4.95/3034-2
The sophisticated gay man knows that he can turn to one authority for answers to virtually any question on the subjects of intimacy and sexual performance. Straight from the pages of *Advocate Men* comes The Sexpert, responding to real-life sexual concerns with uncanny wisdom and a razor wit.

HARD CANDY

DONALD VINING
A GAY DIARY
$8.95/451-8
Donald Vining's *Diary* portrays a long-vanished age and the lifestyle of a gay generation all too frequently forgotten. A touching and revealing volume documenting the surprisingly vibrant culture that existed decades before Stonewall, *A Gay Diary* is not to be missed by anyone interested in gay American history.
"*A Gay Diary* is, unquestionably, the richest historical document of gay male life in the United States that I have ever encountered.... It chronicles a whole life in which homosexuality is but one part and an ever-changing part at that. And, it illuminates a critical period in gay male American history." —*Body Politic*

WALTER HOLLAND
THE MARCH
$6.95/429-1
A moving testament to the power of friendship during even the worst of times. Beginning on a hot summer night in 1980, *The March* revolves around a circle of young gay men, and the many others their lives touch. Over time, each character changes in unexpected ways; lives and loves come together and fall apart, as society itself is horribly altered by the onslaught of AIDS. From the acclaimed author of *A Journal of the Plague Years*.

PATRICK MOORE
IOWA
$6.95/423-2
"Moore is the Tennessee Williams of the nineties—profound intimacy freed in a compelling narrative."
—Karen Finley
"Patrick Moore has...taken the classic story of the Midwest American boyhood that Hemingway, Sinclair Lewis and Sherwood Anderson made classic and he's done it fresh and shiny and relevant to our time. Iowa is full of terrific characters etched in acid-sharp prose, soaked through with just enough ambivalence to make it thoroughly romantic." —Felice Picano
A stunning novel about one gay man's journey into adulthood, and the roads that bring him home again. From the author of the highly praised *This Every Night*.

STAN LEVENTHAL
BARBIE IN BONDAGE
$6.95/415-1
Widely regarded as one of the most refreshing, clear-eyed interpreters of big city gay male life, Leventhal here provides a series of explorations of love and desire between men. Uncompromising, but gentle and generous, *Barbie in Bondage* is a fitting tribute to the late author's unique talents.

BUY ANY 4 BOOKS & CHOOSE 1 ADDITIONAL BOOK, OF EQUAL OR LESSER VALUE, AS YOUR FREE GIFT

HARD CANDY

SKYDIVING ON CHRISTOPHER STREET
$6.95/287-6
"Positively addictive."   —Dennis Cooper
Aside from a hateful job, a hateful apartment, a hateful world and an increasingly hateful lover, life seems, well, all right for the protagonist of Stan Leventhal's latest novel. Having already lost most of his friends to AIDS, how could things get any worse? But things soon do, and he's forced to endure much more....

RED JORDAN AROBATEAU
LUCY AND MICKEY
$6.95/311-2
The story of Mickey—an uncompromising butch—and her long affair with Lucy, the femme she loves.A raw tale of pre-Stonewall lesbian life.
"A necessary reminder to all who blissfully—some may say ignorantly—ride the wave of lesbian chic into the mainstream."   —Heather Findlay

DIRTY PICTURES
$5.95/345-7
"Red Jordan Arobateau is the Thomas Wolfe of lesbian literature... Arobateau's work overflows with vitality and pulsing life. She's a natural—raw talent that is seething, passionate, hard, remarkable."
        —Lillian Faderman, editor of Chloe Plus Olivia
Dirty Pictures is the story of a lonely butch tending bar—and the femme she finally calls her own.

WILLIAM TALSMAN
THE GAUDY IMAGE
$6.95/263-9
"To read The Gaudy Image now...it is to see first-hand the very issues of identity and positionality with which gay men were struggling in the decades before Stonewall. For what Talsman is dealing with...is the very question of how we conceive ourselves gay."
        —from the introduction by Michael Bronski

LARS EIGHNER
GAY COSMOS
$6.95/236-1
A title sure to appeal not only to Eighner's gay fans, but the many converts who first encountered his moving nonfiction work. Praised by the press, Gay Cosmos is an important contribution to the burgeoning area of Gay and Lesbian Studies—and sure to provoke many readers.

FELICE PICANO

THE LURE
$6.95/398-8
"The subject matter, plus the authenticity of Picano's research are, combined, explosive. Felice Picano is one hell of a writer."   —Stephen King
After witnessing a brutal murder, Noel is recruited by the police,to assist as a lure for the killer. Undercover, he moves deep into the freneticism of Manhattan's gay highlife—where he gradually becomes aware of the darker forces at work in his life. In addition to the mystery behind his mission, he begins to recognize changes: in his relationships with the men around him, in himself...

AMBIDEXTROUS
$6.95/275-2
"Deftly evokes those placid Eisenhower years of bicycles, boners, and book reports. Makes us remember what it feels like to be a child..."   —The Advocate
Picano's first "memoir in the form of a novel" tells all: home life, school face-offs, the ingenuous sophistications of his first sexual steps. In three years' time, he's had his first gay fling—and is on his way to becoming the widely praised writer he is today.

MEN WHO LOVED ME
$6.95/274-4
"Zesty...spiked with adventure and romance...a distinguished and humorous portrait of a vanished age."
        —Publishers Weekly
In 1966, Picano abandoned New York, determined to find true love in Europe. When the older and wiser Picano returns to New York at last, he plunges into the city's thriving gay community—experiencing the frenzy and heartbreak that came to define Greenwich Village society in the 1970s.

DIRECT

ROSEBUD

THE ROSEBUD READER
$5.95/319-8
Rosebud has contributed greatly to the burgeoning genre of lesbian erotica—to the point that authors like Lindsay Welsh, Aarona Griffin and Valentina Cilescu are among the hottest and most closely watched names in lesbian and gay publishing. Here are the finest moments from Rosebud's contemporary classics.

K. T. BUTLER
TOOLS OF THE TRADE
$5.95/420-8
A sparkling mix of lesbian erotica and humor. An encounter with ice cream, cappuccino and chocolate cake; an affair with a complete stranger; a pair of faulty handcuffs; and love on a drafting table. Seventeen tales.

ALISON TYLER
DARK ROOM: AN ONLINE ADVENTURE
$6.50/455-0
Dani, a successful photographer, can't bring herself to face the death of her lover, Kate. An ambitious journalist, Kate was found mysteriously murdered, leaving her lover with only fond memories of a too-brief relationship. Determined to keep the memory of her lover alive, Dani goes online under Kate's screen alias—and begins to uncover the truth behind the crime that has torn her world apart.

BLUE SKY SIDEWAYS & OTHER STORIES
$6.50/394-5
A variety of women, and their many breathtaking experiences with lovers, friends—and even the occasional sexy stranger. From blossoming young beauties to fearless vixens, Tyler finds the sexy pleasures of everyday life.

DIAL "L" FOR LOVELESS
$5.95/386-4
Meet Katrina Loveless—a private eye talented enough to give Sam Spade a run for his money. In her first case, Katrina investigates a murder implicating a host of society's darlings—including wealthy Tessa and Baxter Saint Claire, and the lovely, tantalizing, infamous Geneva twins. Loveless untangles the mess— while working herself into a variety of highly compromising knots with the many lovelies who cross her path!

THE VIRGIN
$5.95/379-1
Veronica answers a personal ad in the "Women Seeking Women" category—and discovers a whole sensual world she never knew existed! And she never dreamed she'd be prized as a virgin all over again, by someone who would deflower her with a passion no man could ever show....

THE BLUE ROSE
$5.95/335-X
The tale of a modern sorority—fashioned after a Victorian girls' school. Ignited to the heights of passion by erotic tales of the Victorian age, a group of lusty young women are encouraged to act out their forbidden fantasies—all under the tutelage of Mistresses Emily and Justine, two avid practitioners of hard-core discipline!

LOVECHILD

GAG
$5.95/369-4
From New York's poetry scene comes this explosive volume of work from one of the bravest, most cutting young writers you'll ever encounter. The poems in Gag take on American hypocrisy with uncommon energy, and announce Lovechild as a writer of unforgettable rage.

ELIZABETH OLIVER
THE SM MURDER: MURDER AT ROMAN HILL
$5.95/353-8
Intrepid lesbian P.I.s Leslie Patrick and Robin Penny take on a really hot case: the murder of the notorious Felicia Roman. The circumstances of the crime lead the pair on an excursion through the leatherdyke underground, where motives—and desires—run deep. But as Leslie and Robin soon find, every woman harbors her own closely guarded secret....

PAGAN DREAMS
$5.95/295-7
Cassidy and Samantha plan a vacation at a secluded bed-and-breakfast, hoping for a little personal time alone. Their hostess, however, has different plans. The lovers are plunged into a world of dungeons and pagan rites, as Anastasia steals Samantha for her own.

ROSEBUD

SUSAN ANDERS

CITY OF WOMEN
$5.95/375-9
Stories dedicated to women and the passions that draw them together. Designed strictly for the sensual pleasure of women, these tales are set to ignite flames of passion from coast to coast.

PINK CHAMPAGNE
$5.95/282-5
Tasty, torrid tales of butch/femme couplings. Tough as nails or soft as silk, these women seek out their antitheses, intent on working out the details of their own personal theory of difference.

ANONYMOUS

LAVENDER ROSE
$4.95/208-6
A classic collection of lesbian literature. From the writings of Sappho, Queen of the island Lesbos, to the turn-of-the-century *Black Book of Lesbianism*; from *Tips to Maidens* to *Crimson Hairs*, a recent lesbian saga—here are the great but little-known lesbian writings and revelations. A one volume survey of hot lesbian writing.

LAURA ANTONIOU, EDITOR

LEATHERWOMEN
$4.95/3095-4
These fantasies, from the pens of new or emerging authors, break every rule imposed on women's fantasies. The hottest stories from some of today's newest and most outrageous writers make this an unforgettable exploration of the female libido.

LEATHERWOMEN II
$4.95/229-9
Laura Antoniou turns an editor's discerning eye to the writings of women on the edge—resulting in a collection sure to ignite libidinal flames. Leave taboos behind, because these Leatherwomen know no limits....

AARONA GRIFFIN

PASSAGE AND OTHER STORIES
$4.95/3057-1
An S/M romance. Lovely Nina is frightened by her lesbian passions, until she finds herself infatuated with a woman she spots at a local café. One night Nina follows her, and finds herself enmeshed in an endless maze leading to a world where women test the edges of sexuality and power.

VALENTINA CILESCU

**MY LADY'S PLEASURE:
WOMAN WITH A MAID VOLUME I**
$5.95/412-7
Dr. Claudia Dungarrow, a lovely, powerful, but mysterious figure at St. Matilda's College, comes face to face with desires that might prove the undoing of an ordinary woman. For when her hungers lead her to attempt seducing the virginal Elizabeth Stanbridge, she sets off a chain of events that eventually ruins her career. But Claudia vows revenge—and has it in her power to make her foes pay deliciously....

THE ROSEBUD SUTRA
$4.95/242-6
"Women are hardly ever known in their true light, though they may love others, or become indifferent towards them, may give them delight, or abandon them, or may extract from them all the wealth that they possess." So says *The Rosebud Sutra*—a volume promising women's inner secrets. One woman learns to use these secrets in a quest for pleasure with a succession of lady loves....

THE HAVEN
$4.95/165-9
J craves domination, and her perverse appetites lead her to the Haven: the isolated sanctuary Ros and Annie call home. Soon J forces her way into the couple's world, bringing unspeakable lust and cruelty into their lives.

MISTRESS MINE
$5.95/445-3
Sophia Cranleigh sits in prison, accused of authoring the "obscene" *Mistress Mine*. What she has done, however, is merely chronicle the events of her life—to the outrage of many. For Sophia has led no ordinary life, but has slaved and suffered—deliciously—under the hand of the notorious Mistress Malin. How long had she languished under the dominance of this incredible beauty?

LINDSAY WELSH

NASTY PERSUASIONS
$6.50/436-4
A hot peek into the behind-the-scenes operations of Rough Trade—one of the world's most famous lesbian clubs. Join Slash, Ramone, Cherry and many others as they bring one another to the height of torturous ecstasy—all in the name of keeping Rough Trade the premier name in sexy entertainment for women.

MASQUERADE DIRECT

ROSEBUD

MILITARY SECRETS
$5.95/397-X
Colonel Candice Sproule heads a highly specialized boot camp. Assisted by three dominatrix sergeants, Col. Sproule takes on the talented submissives sent to her by secret military contacts. Then comes Jesse—whose pleasure in being served matches the Colonel's own. This new recruit sets off fireworks in the barracks—and beyond....

ROMANTIC ENCOUNTERS
$5.95/359-7
Beautiful Julie, the most powerful editor of romance novels in the industry, spends her days igniting women's passions through books—and her nights fulfilling those needs with a variety of lovers. Finally, through a sizzling series of coincidences, Julie's two worlds come together explosively!

THE BEST OF LINDSAY WELSH
$5.95/368-6
A collection of this popular writer's best work. This author was one of Rosebud's early bestsellers, and remains highly popular. A sampler set to introduce some of the hottest lesbian erotica to a wider audience.

NECESSARY EVIL
$5.95/277-9
What's a girl to do? When her Mistress proves too systematic, too by-the-book, one lovely submissive takes the ultimate chance—choosing and creating a Mistress who'll fulfill her heart's desire. Little did she know how difficult it would be—and, in the end, rewarding....

A VICTORIAN ROMANCE
$5.95/365-1
Lust-letters from the road. A young Englishwoman realizes her dream—a trip abroad under the guidance of her eccentric maiden aunt. Soon, the young but blossoming Elaine comes to discover her own sexual talents, as a hot-blooded Parisian named Madelaine takes her Sapphic education in hand.

A CIRCLE OF FRIENDS
$4.95/250-7
The story of a remarkable group of women. The women pair off to explore all the possibilities of lesbian passion, until finally it seems that there is nothing—and no one—they have not dabbled in.

BAD HABITS
$5.95/446-1
What does one do with a poorly trained slave? Break her of her bad habits, of course! The story of the ultimate finishing school, Bad Habits was an immediate favorite with women nationwide. "Talk about passing the wet test!... If you like hot, lesbian erotica, run—don't walk—and pick up a copy of *Bad Habits.*"
—*Lambda Book Report*

ANNABELLE BARKER
MOROCCO
$4.95/148-9
A luscious young woman stands to inherit a fortune—if she can only withstand the ministrations of her cruel guardian until her twentieth birthday. With two months left, Lila makes a bold bid for freedom, only to find that liberty has its own excruciating and delicious price....

A.L. REINE
DISTANT LOVE & OTHER STORIES
$4.95/3056-3
In the title story, Leah Michaels and her lover, Ranelle, have had four years of blissful, smoldering passion together. When Ranelle is out of town, Leah records an audio "Valentine:" a cassette filled with erotic reminiscences....

MICHAEL FORD, EDITOR
**ONCE UPON A TIME:
EROTIC FAIRY TALES FOR WOMEN**
$12.95/449-6
How relevant to contemporary lesbians are the lessons of these age-old tales? The contributors to *Once Upon a Time*—some of the biggest names in contemporary lesbian literature—retell their favorite fairy tales, adding their own surprising—and sexy—twists. *Once Upon a Time* is sure to be one of contemporary lesbian literature's classic collections. Includes work by Dorothy Allison, Red Jordan Arobateau, and many of today's most provocative writers.

**HAPPILY EVER AFTER:
EROTIC FAIRY TALES FOR MEN**
$12.95/450-X
A hefty volume of bedtime stories Mother Goose never thought to write down. Adapting some of childhood's most beloved tales for the adult gay reader, the contributors to *Happily Ever After* dig up the subtext of these hitherto "innocent" diversions—adding some surprises of their own along the way. Includes stories by Larry Townsend, Michael Lassell, Bruce Benderson and others.

CHARLES HENRI FORD & PARKER TYLER
THE YOUNG AND EVIL
$12.95/431-3
"*The Young and Evil* creates [its] generation as *This Side of Paradise* by Fitzgerald created his generation."
—Gertrude Stein
"The first candid, gloves-off account of more or less professional young homosexuals."
—Louis Kronenberger, *New Republic*
Originally published in 1933, *The Young and Evil* was an immediate sensation due to its unprecedented portrayal of young gay artists living in New York's notorious Greenwich Village. From flamboyant drag balls to squalid bohemian flats, these characters followed love and art wherever it led them—with a frankness that had the novel banned for many years. This volume includes a biographical introduction detailing the many ways in which the authors' lives paralleled those of their characters, as well as rare photography and artwork from the period. An essential look at the gay past.

SHAR REDNOUR, EDITOR
VIRGIN TERRITORY
$12.95/457-7
Writing by women about their first-time erotic experiences with other women. From the longings and ecstasies of awakening dykes to the sometimes awkward pleasures of sexual experimentation on the edge, each of these true stories reveals a different, radical perspective on one of the most traditional subjects around: virginity.

HEATHER FINDLAY, EDITOR
**A MOVEMENT OF EROS:
25 YEARS OF LESBIAN EROTICA**
$12.95/421-6
One of the most scintillating overviews of lesbian erotic writing ever published. Heather Findlay has assembled a roster of stellar talents, each represented by their best work. Tracing the course of the genre from its pre-Stonewall roots to its current renaissance, Findlay examines such diverse talents as Jewelle Gomez, Chrystos, Pat Califia and Linda Smukler, placing them within the context of lesbian community and politics.

MICHAEL BRONSKI, EDITOR
**TAKING LIBERTIES: GAY MEN'S ESSAYS
ON POLITICS, CULTURE AND SEX**
$12.95/456-9
"*Taking Liberties* offers undeniable proof of a heady, sophisticated, diverse new culture of gay intellectual debate. I cannot recommend it too highly."
—Christopher Bram
Taking Liberties brings together some of the most divergent views on the state of contemporary gay male culture published in recent years. Michael Bronski here presents some of the community's foremost essayists weighing in on such slippery topics as outing, masculine identity, pornography, the pedophile movement, community definition, political strategy—and much more.

FLASHPOINT: GAY MALE SEXUAL WRITING
$12.95/424-0
A collection of the most provocative testaments to gay eros. Michael Bronski presents over twenty of the genre's best writers, exploring areas such as Enlightenment, True Life Adventures and more. Sure to be one of the most talked about and influential volumes ever dedicated to the exploration of gay sexuality.

EURYDICE

F/32
$10.95/350-3

"It's wonderful to see a woman...celebrating her body and her sexuality by creating a fabulous and funny tale."
—Kathy Acker

With the story of Ela (whose name is a pseudonym for orgasm), Eurydice won the National Fiction competition sponsored by Fiction Collective Two and Illinois State University. A funny, disturbing quest for unity, *f/32* prompted Frederic Tuten to proclaim "almost any page...redeems us from the anemic writing and banalities we have endured in the past decade..."

CECILIA TAN, EDITOR
SM VISIONS: THE BEST OF CIRCLET PRESS
$10.95/339-2

"Fabulous books! There's nothing else like them."
—Susie Bright, *Best American Erotica* and *Herotica 3*
Circlet Press, devoted exclusively to the erotic science fiction and fantasy genre, is now represented by the best of its very best: *SM Visions*—sure to be one of the most thrilling and eye-opening rides through the erotic imagination ever published.

MICHAEL LASSELL
THE HARD WAY
$12.95/231-0

"Lassell is a master of the necessary word. In an age of tepid and whining verse, his bawdy and bittersweet songs are like a plunge in cold champagne." —Paul Monette
The first collection of renowned gay writer Michael Lassell's poetry, fiction and essays. As much a chronicle of post-Stonewall gay life as a compendium of a remarkable writer's work.

AMARANTHA KNIGHT, EDITOR
LOVE BITES
$12.95/234-5

A volume of tales dedicated to legend's sexiest demon— the Vampire. Includes many writers who helped legitimize the erotic-horror genre, including Ron Dee, Nancy A. Collins, Nancy Kilpatrick, Lois Tilton and David Aaron Clark. Not only the finest collection of erotic horror available— but a virtual who's who of promising new talent. A must for fans of both the horror and erotic genres.

LOOKING FOR MR. PRESTON
$23.95/288-4

Edited by Laura Antoniou, *Looking for Mr. Preston* includes work by Lars Eighner, Pat Califia, Michael Bronski, Joan Nestle, and others who contributed interviews, essays and personal reminiscences of John Preston—a man whose career spanned the industry. Preston was the author of over twenty books, and edited many more. Ten percent of the proceeds from sale of the book will go to the AIDS Project of Southern Maine, for which Preston served as President of the Board.

SAMUEL R. DELANY
THE MOTION OF LIGHT IN WATER
$12.95/133-0

"A very moving, intensely fascinating literary biography from an extraordinary writer. Thoroughly admirable candor and luminous stylistic precision; the artist as a young man and a memorable picture of an age." —William Gibson
Award-winning author Samuel R. Delany's autobiography covers the early years of one of science fiction's most important voices. *The Motion of Light in Water* follows Delany from his early marriage to the poet Marilyn Hacker, through the publication of his first, groundbreaking work. Delany paints a vivid and compelling picture of New York's East Village in the early '60s—a time of unprecedented social transformation.

THE MAD MAN
$23.95/193-4/hardcover

Delany's fascinating examination of human desire. For his thesis, graduate student John Marr researches the life and work of the brilliant Timothy Hasler: a philosopher whose career was cut tragically short over a decade earlier. Marr soon begins to believe that Hasler's death might hold some key to his own life as a gay man in the age of AIDS.
"What Delany has done here is take the ideas of the Marquis de Sade one step further, by filtering extreme and obsessive sexual behavior through the sieve of post-modern experience...." —*Lambda Book Report*
"Delany develops an insightful dichotomy between [his protagonist]'s two worlds: the one of cerebral philosophy and dry academia, the other of heedless, 'impersonal' obsessive sexual extremism. When these worlds finally collide ... the novel achieves a surprisingly satisfying resolution...."
—*Publishers Weekly*

ORDERING IS EASY!

MC/VISA orders can be placed by calling our toll-free number
PHONE 800-375-2356 / FAX 212 986-7355
or mail this coupon to:
MASQUERADE DIRECT
DEPT. BMRB76   **801 2ND AVE., NY, NY 10017**

**BUY ANY FOUR BOOKS AND CHOOSE ONE ADDITIONAL BOOK,
OF EQUAL OR LESSER VALUE, AS YOUR FREE GIFT.**

QTY.	TITLE	NO.	PRICE
			FREE
			FREE

WE NEVER SELL, GIVE OR TRADE ANY CUSTOMER'S NAME.

BMRB76

	SUBTOTAL	
POSTAGE and HANDLING	
TOTAL	

In the U.S., please add $1.50 for the first book and 75¢ for each additional book; in Canada, add $2.00 for the first book and $1.25 for each additional book. Foreign countries: add $4.00 for the first book and $2.00 for each additional book. No C.O.D. orders. Please make all checks payable to Masquerade Books. Payable in U.S. currency only. New York state residents add 8.25% sales tax. Please allow 4-6 weeks for delivery.

NAME _____

ADDRESS _____

CITY _____ STATE _____ ZIP _____

TEL ( ) _____

PAYMENT: ☐ CHECK ☐ MONEY ORDER ☐ VISA ☐ MC

CARD NO. _____ EXP. DATE _____